Paul Pa[rk]

"Paul Park is one of the most gifted and
subtle story writers I know."
—Jonathan Lethem

"Entering a Paul Park universe means slipping into an eerily
compelling plane where nearly palpable visions transform as
disturbing as the images in a sexually charged fever dream."
—*Publishers Weekly*

"Paul Park's short stories are blunt, funny, distressing,
strange, true—all these qualities, often all at once."
—Kim Stanley Robinson

"Genre writing is both a liberation and a confinement. If those
who don't read science fiction could discover Paul Park, they
would find a writer as complex, as skillful, as ambitious, and
as many-faceted as any they would find under any rubric."
—John Crowley

A City Made of Words

of Words

plus

PM PRESS OUTSPOKEN AUTHORS SERIES

PM PRESS OUTSPOKEN AUTHORS SERIES

A City Made of Words

plus

Climate Change

plus

A Resistance to Theory

and much more

Paul Park

PM PRESS | 2019

"A Short History of Science Fiction" was first published in the collection *Other Stories* (PS Publishing, 2015).

"A Resistance to Theory" was first published online at Conjunctions.com, November 2014.

"Blind Spot" was first published in "Other Aliens," *Conjunctions 67*, Fall 2016.

"Creative Nonfiction" was first published in *Asimov's* 42, no. 5–6, May/June 2018.

"A Homily for Good Friday" was delivered at St. John's Episcopal Church in Williamstown, MA.

"A Conversation with the Author" and "Climate Change" are original to this volume.

ISBN: 978-1-62963-642-9
LCCN: 2018949075

Cover design by John Yates/www.stealworks.com
Author photo by Deborah Brothers

CONTENTS

A Short History of Science Fiction, or The Microscopic Eye

This course was taken with John Palmer, and the true
secret of his mysterious power of vision detected in
an instant. . . . The eye examined was exceedingly
flat, very thin, with large iris, flat lens, immense
petira, and wonderfully dilated pupil. The effect
of the shape was at once apparent. It was utterly
impossible to see any object with distinctness at
any distance short of many thousands of miles.
—W.H. Rhodes, "The Telescopic Eye," 1876

HE WAS THERE WHEN I arrived in the morning, there when I
left at night: an old man who had staked out as his place of
business a square yard of sidewalk next to the revolving door,
in which location he sold pencils and matches when he had
them. Or if he did not he stood there anyway, marking time
as did so many in those days, dressed in a threadbare blue
suit and dirty collar, wearing around his neck a neatly lettered
placard—"Blind."

All winter and into spring, in downtown San Francisco I
saw him every day outside the bank where I worked. At that

time I had taken up the habit of attending more than the usual complement of religious services. Nowadays I don't participate at all. But that year I was a vestryman at an Episcopal chapel, and for Holy Week I was in charge of the Maundy Thursday celebration, during which our rector intended to wash the feet of twelve lucky indigents. Our chapel sponsored a soup kitchen where I could have easily found the requisite number or indeed any number at all, the evening crowd outside the basement was so large. But I was not drawn to these citizens, farmers from Texas and Oklahoma who had come to San Francisco as a last resort, as if the city were a mesh at the bottom of a drain. No matter how poor they were, they could always find money for tobacco and alcohol. Their leathery skins and flat accents were alien to me, and I was concerned, also, by the prospect of awakening any hope at all in them, any expectation of special treatment or potential employment, by their participation in what was after all a useless kind of spectacle.

Instead, I imagined I could explain myself better to the match-seller outside my building, where I worked as a loans officer. His clothes marked him as a city resident, and his voice as he thanked me on some mornings for my nickel or even once my dime seemed to suggest a native of California. A deserving unfortunate, I thought, the kind of person our Lord specifically enjoins us to protect.

You will forgive me if I speak ironically. I was just about at the end of my tether, and I thought his blind eyes would register no disappointment. I did not ask him on Monday or on Tuesday, but on Wednesday evening I stopped in front of him to stammer out my request. The crowds in the streets had diminished, and we stood alone beside the granite front.

He raised his face to look at me, a gaunt face commanded by enormous, empty, bulging, malformed eyes. But for a moment I wondered if he was blind at all.

I introduced myself.

"John Palmer," he said. He was past sixty, I thought, perhaps closer to three score and ten. "Culp Hill," he suggested when I asked where he was from, a neighborhood that, with his name and the calm gaze of his enormous eyes seemed to tear something from my memory.

"Sir, I am not a beggar or a vagrant. That makes it hard for me to accurately represent one of the Apostles, if I understand you . . ." He continued on like that, his voice gentle and good-natured, but by that time I had stopped listening. His eyes shone like lenses and I peered down into them. Could it be?

I interrupted him. "You're Johnny Palmer," I cried. "You're the boy who saw the men in the moon."

He winced. But I ignored his stricken look as I continued. "You're the boy who saw the cities on Mars. My father saved the clippings. Your picture was in the newspapers."

Laboriously, insincerely, he smiled. "Not a boy, sir."

Someone had turned on the lights in the restaurant across the street. The blind man shrugged, opened his palms apologetically. "I believed it," I cried. "I believed every word. Oceans of quicksilver, colored creatures sliding back and forth across the horizon line. And then Percival Lowell and his Martian canali. We thought he had confirmed your observations."

"Percival who?"

He kept on smiling that same false, ingratiating smile. But at moments I thought I could detect something else, some wisp of a genuine feeling that was both melancholy and reflective.

But perhaps I was mistaken, and it was my mood that fluctuated as I recalled my childish hopes for worlds beyond this one, unimaginable frontiers.

In 1876, when he was nine years old, Johnny Palmer was examined at his parents' house on Culp Hill, in what was then the south end of the city. A committee from the School of Sciences, as well as several independent oculists, had subsequently published their results. Nature had flattened the boy's eyeballs to a wonderful degree, they claimed, so as to cause a type of presbyopia or farsightedness. His mother had thought him blind from birth, though sensitive to light. It was only when he turned his gaze into the face of the full moon that he was able to see clearly, at a distance of 240,000 miles.

"They turned in circles," I said brokenly. "The lunarians, you called them. Millions of them together made patterns of polygonal shapes. I remember—"

"Do you? I don't. Not anymore."

His face, rinsed in the orange light from across the street, seemed beyond hope. His chin was covered in pale stubble, and there was a hole in the brim of his hat. His eyes gleamed like lanterns in his wasted face. "Please, sir," he said finally. "If you have a dime, I could get something to eat."

I looked away. A taxicab was prowling down the center of the street. I put up my hand. "So it was all lies," I murmured. "I suppose it must have been all lies. No one believes it anymore."

But then I wondered why he seemed so sad. As if to duplicate my thoughts, he murmured, "No, I don't think so. I don't think it was lies."

Always a sucker, I waved the taxi on and then turned back to him. "It's just I can't remember," he said.

But at that moment, as it happened, I looked up to see the nimbus of the moon off toward the east, a patch of light between the buildings. So excited I was, I grasped hold of the man's sleeve and pulled him down the street, and in the larger sky by the cigar stand at the corner I could see the half moon above me, caught in a net of wires.

"Look," I said.

I let go of him, and he stood smoothing his cuffs, staring down at the clogged gutter. "I don't remember," he said. And when he raised his face, I thought the changing light had bleached away all trace of resentment or ingratiation. "They took me away."

"Who did?"

"I don't know. I was nine years old. Ten years old, eleven. They took me places all the time, asked me questions. Examined me. So at first I didn't realize they were different. They had foreign voices, but I didn't guess. Not at first. How could I guess? They came to my house at night, took me from my mother—I thought it was the East Coast. New York City, some such place. But it was a long way on the train, a longer way on the cold ship, and when I came out—do you know what? Up above my head I could see the entire promontory. I could see the city, right here. The whole length of Market Street and all the people, for the first time. Sausalito, across the gate. Like a map come alive. My parents' house, and all down the coast when the clouds pulled away. I could look at it forever."

There was a bus, a bray of horns. There were the headlamps of the oncoming traffic.

"I don't understand," I said.

But then as I grasped the significance of his remarks, I found myself trembling. "You are lying to me," I said.

He smiled, shrugged, made that peculiar gesture with his hands. I felt like striking him, old, blind, and hungry though he was. Fleetingly I wondered if the chapel was open, and I could run over there and sit down on one of the wooden benches near the altar, though off to one side. I'd sit under the stone vault and watch the candles.

"Tell me," I said, always a sucker. And he stood in the roadway as the people hurried past, and he told me how the people there had built some kind of observatory for him. When the round balloon of the Earth floated above the horizon, he had described it to them as carefully as he could.

"How did they bring you to that place?" I asked.

"I don't know."

"What was it like?"

He smiled. "It was cold. I couldn't see them. I couldn't see anything. You must understand."

By this time I had brought him back up the street to the restaurant. I had sat him down and ordered him the blue-plate special, which was sausages and beans. He ripped pieces of bread from the loaf. He told me how long it was since he had eaten a hot meal. This was not the kind of food that I enjoyed or trusted, so I drank water. I have always had a sensitive stomach, and I disliked the sight of the cooks and their stoves, the flare of their greasy fires. The place was so small, the kitchen was in plain view. Palmer was lucky he was blind, I thought, and then chastised myself for being so uncharitable. But I was angry, more and more angry as he kept on talking. Did the fellow take me for a fool? Men from Mars! How had they come here? Why had they taken him and brought him back? What language did they speak?

"I was no more use to them," he said between mouthfuls. How sad he seemed! "It was because my eyes were changing. I have a medical condition," he said, raising his face, staring across the seamed and pitted table, his eyes bulging out at me. A medical condition, I thought—that was the least of it! "Progressive myopia," he said mildly. "It took a long time to develop."

I should say so! I sat back in my chair. He pushed his empty plate away, sipped from his coffee cup, put it down as well. He wiped his lips, refolded his napkin, while at the same time he was telling me about a happy portion of his life when his vision was corrected with ordinary spectacles, the lenses weaker every year. Then for a day or so he could see the faces of his wife and children unaided and at any distance. This was a contented time, between the earthquake and the great war. I also remembered it.

"And now?" I asked. I couldn't help myself.

For an answer, he lowered his face toward the surface of the table. I thought for a moment that, sated, he was going to put his cheek down on the filthy surface and fall asleep. I thought also it was possible he had gulled me this whole time. Drunk all day, perhaps, now he was collapsing to unconsciousness. Except he pressed the point of his nose into the wood, and then turned his head so that the lens of his eye was no more than a quarter of an inch from the grimy tabletop. "Do you know what I see?" he asked.

"God, don't tell me," I said.

But he paid no attention. He could not keep from telling me. Nor did his tone contain any lingering admixture of diffidence or apology. Instead, he seemed almost proud of his disease, which had progressed so far as to enable him to see entire villages and municipalities of microbes, armies of them, serried ranks, marching and seething over the greasy plain. "They cannot be still," he said, describing what he saw, a revolution or a civil war, a navy sailing on a pool of grease, a citadel succumbing under a mass of tiny assailants. "Fat ones, thin ones," he said, seizing hold of my hand in an unbreakable grip, pulling it toward him and lowering his eye almost to the surface of my skin. "I see them," he said. And I would not have been able to let go except he let me go, let me leave him, finally, and stumble out into the street, where I stood wiping my fingers in my handkerchief and rubbing my palms together.

Blind Spot

"THE THING IS, YOU can't tell the difference. At least not from the outside. Because of interbreeding and genetic manipulation."

"What are you saying now?"

"It's a moral difference. That and perception. They have sharp ears, for one thing. Hear things from far away. Walk past a house from the outside, just along the garden walk, hear what people say around corners. Hear people in their bedrooms."

"That's quite funny, the thing you do."

"What?"

"Using the same word in different ways so close together. From the outside. Difference. Walk."

"That's what I meant," he said. "They're very sensitive."

By "garden walk" he meant the crazy paving next to the stone wall, chest high. There were hollyhocks. By "around corners" he meant because the bedroom faced the street. The stone wall was in the back. You got to it across the meadow through the butter-and-eggs.

"Please go on."

"Because they are reptilian, originally, they have a nictitating membrane. Some of them do. It's very quick. It slides across. Yellowish, I suppose."

Or else he meant because the bedroom was on the first floor, the windowsill high above the ground. The house itself was yellow stucco and a tile roof.

"No."

"I'm telling you. It was in the book. Long tongues. They smell through their tongues."

Roses among the hollyhocks around a corner of the wall.

"And you can't figure out by looking?"

"What do you mean? They can see through walls."

"I mean by looking at them."

"Not anymore. It's been too long. They could be you or me. Thirty-six hundred years is their planet's orbit, and now the first ones have assimilated. But guess what?" he said. "They're coming back."

An older man, he stood by the window looking out onto the street. Gauze curtains. The other one lay on his back across the saffron bedspread. Tufted chenille. He smiled. "Go on," he said, "pull it again. Pull it harder."

"I'm telling you, they started everything. This was in Mesopotamia. Before that we were just living in caves. I'm speaking of the wheel, written languages, agriculture. They were technologically advanced. They'd have to be, coming from outer space. But not just that. They could see the whole past, the whole future, the whole world laid out. Worlds beyond worlds. Like it was written in a book."

The older man's name was Roland Styce. He had been born in Wales. He was a big man, unshaven. For seven years his psychiatrist had been prescribing him a combination of serotonin inhibitors to treat his symptoms, most recently fluoxetine, with an antipsychotic (Zyprexa) to stabilize his moods. Sometimes, though, he tried to do without. As now, for example. Since his mid-twenties he had worked as a teller in a bank. He was forty-seven.

The younger man lay propped up on his elbows. He had less time behind him. And even barring any sort of cataclysmic interruption, he had less in front of him as well. Soon, he would work another tattoo into the pattern on the inside of his left arm, an image taken from a tarot deck. He would spend six years in jail. Soon after, he'd be dead.

Even excepting some sort of violent interruption, he would be dead in nine years' time. He would die in hospital, in the city of Leeds, not a hundred kilometers from the stucco house. Leeds is in the center of the United Kingdom. Above it, in the night sky, there is no trace of the twelfth planet as it approaches perihelion. You can scarcely see the stars.

"What's the problem, then? Maybe they can help us sort out some of this mess."

"I wouldn't be so sure," said Roland Styce. "They don't care anything about us. They're very cruel."

Despite his years of service to the Midland Trust, he had never once been promoted, because of his low intellect. His flesh had a pasty look to it. His hands were large and fat, with fingers like moist rolls of uncooked dough, painted with egg white, dusted with red spots of pepper, and then sprinkled unaccountably with hair, according to the recipe of some deranged pastry chef. They were a masturbator's hands. No one touched them voluntarily to say hello: His superiors in the bank (he had no inferiors) avoided greeting him, preferring instead to touch him vaguely on the shoulder, which, though disgusting in its own right, a wobbly pudding of tufted flesh, at least had the advantage of being clothed. No one had liked him in a long time.

He was the kind of man who said most things twice. "We're like nothing to them. Every single one of us could die."

"I don't get that," said the younger man. "You said we were all mixed in now. Interbred for two hundred generations . . ."

"They don't care about themselves!" Styce interrupted. "They're cannibals on Niburu. That's their home planet. We were nothing but slaves to them, slaves to mine gold, which they used to make heat and light. Most of them were eight feet tall. We worshipped them as gods. You can see in those Sumerian bas-reliefs in the British Museum.

"I read about it in a book called *The Twelfth Planet*," he continued after a pause.

The younger man grimaced, then stretched out his jaw and snapped his teeth together. Yellow and discolored, they made a satisfying snap. In nine years, barring any sort of incomprehensible calamity, he would die of an intracranial neoplasm in the city of Leeds. "So we'll have to fight them, then," he said. "We're not as helpless this time around."

"Perhaps not. They do have an advantage, though."

"What's that?"

"They can read minds."

All day he'd been afraid. That morning he had woken as if under a dim, inchoate nebula of doubt, riven with anxiety as if by spears of light. "The Twelfth Planet," he had muttered to himself as he had blundered out of bed into his slippers: This mania of his, gathering now, was a way of struggling against these feelings by a process of deflection, the way you might squeeze your thumb with a nutcracker as a cure for seasickness.

The younger man saw nothing of this. He saw an older fellow, overweight, standing by the window, just beginning to unbutton his shirt. He scarcely listened when the fellow spoke: "The light is dim where they are. Most of the time, except for the foci of the ellipse, you see, they don't have a setting or a rising sun. They seed their atmosphere with molecules of gold, which reflect light from the rifts in their own oceans, the volcanic activity there. The light is always dim, so they don't sleep."

"What are you, an astronomer, then?"

"No, I work at the Royal Bank of Scotland. I'm the chief teller there in town," which was a pointless lie.

"That's all right," said the younger man.

Roland Styce turned toward him. "There is one advantage, though. A blind spot, if you will."

"What's that?"

"It's because of the way they reproduce in an abnormal way. Because of their reptilian nature, and the way they go into a stasis without sleeping. They don't understand anything about love. You know, what we call love. It's like a blind spot. It enrages them."

"Well, that's all right, then."

The garden wall was low, about five feet, and faced with yellow stone. Beyond it, and beyond the raised beds, the grass spread flat and featureless to the back steps, like a lava field abraded into greenness under the acid rain.

The door was locked and barred. Solid oak, imported from Poland. On the other side, a tufted oriental carpet ran the length of the hall, various living rooms on either side. Mr. Styce had inherited the house from his mother in 2016. She had died of an aneurism that same summer.

Along the way down the corridor, you smelled a number of competing fragrances, more intense at intervals if you licked your lips. Sawdust. Lemon furniture polish. Then you came past the kitchen's open door, the sealed cabinets full of sealed jars of Indian chutneys and pickles. A bowl of onions. Some wilted flowers. The stair rose up and turned a corner to the first floor. A skylight shone west above the landing, and the air was pricked with motes of gold.

These people, these creatures, sealed up like jars or cans, struggling to see or know or understand even a little bit, how could you not open them and spill them out? Caught in a spatial moment, how could you not twist them, stretch them out beyond their capabilities? Some broke open and rose up higher and higher until you could see the world and time and space spread away.

Yet up there, behind that closed door, two men embraced on a yellow bed.

A Conversation with the Author

Question:
Elsewhere you have complained, or almost complained, about the traditional fiction-writing workshop, in which a group of students, selected on the basis of a writing sample, presents a story for critique. Each student says a chunk of words about it, and then the instructor sums up. You've suggested, or at least thought about suggesting, that although this method serves the needs of young writers craving an audience, it isn't really the best method of teaching this particular discipline. Would you care to elaborate?

Answer:
"Once I taught writing in an expensive college. I imagined it was an important subject. For one thing, I told my colleagues in the English Department, how could you claim that you were competent to analyze and interpret other people's stories and novels without any idea of how they were constructed?

"Mostly I told them this internally, or as soon as they'd stopped listening, or sometimes while they slept. I used a low, quiet, breathless tone of voice. In addition, I whispered, you can't or shouldn't write any kind of nonfiction without some knowledge of the basics of storytelling. How do we know? It's because even mediocre novelists are good essayists. The reverse is never true.

"And it's easy to see why: both stories and essays consist of plotted, causally related sequences of events. The basic arsenal of the fiction writer—how to control atmosphere, how to build suspense, how to reach a conclusion that is neither adventitious nor predictable—will make even the weakest argument impregnable.

"The gifts of a science fiction writer are particularly useful in this regard. Science fiction stories usually carry an unusual burden of exposition. And they usually include either an overt or implied thesis, often one of each."

After this harangue, the author lapsed briefly into silence. But already I was sick of his nonsense. He was someone we'd picked up during one of our sweeps of the docks. He'd been apprehended lurking underneath the pier and then relocated to a camp for displaced persons. Now we'd brought him in for questioning. Under the circumstances, his well-rehearsed sentences seemed delusional. "I've scarcely dinged the surface," he went on. "There are many other benefits to the study of story writing. I would often notice during the first six weeks, around the time we started to discuss point of view, that my students seemed happier, somehow. In some cases, their skin had cleared up. They had found girlfriends or boyfriends. During office hours, they would admit they had stopped taking their anxiety medications and were suffering no adverse effects. After my unit on techniques of characterization, a young woman whom I had last seen in a wheelchair came in haltingly to class, on crutches. A week later, after my seminar on voice, she had graduated to a cane."

He was making a joke, I decided. "Mirabile dictu," I said. He also, as it happened, was in a wheelchair, his arms strapped down, which was why, perhaps, the memory had occurred to him.

"I am willing to concede the value of fiction writing as a discipline," I continued in all sincerity. "Perhaps I should rephrase my question. Is there anything you were unable to accomplish in your class?"

I sat across a narrow metal table, recording our conversation on a tablet. At the same time I sketched him with the stylus, according to my habit—the front of his shirt, his shoulders. I am not good at faces, so I hadn't attempted that.

"Well, there is one thing," he said. "A detail."

"Let me guess," I said.

But he interrupted me. "I wasn't able to improve their actual skills. Their stories never got any better."

I took particular pains with the button-down collar points of his shirt, though I omitted some of the dirt. The cave-like opening to the collar itself, I filled with careful cross-hatching. This was in lieu of any head or neck.

"Let me sum up," I said. "According to you, the study of fiction writing is important to literary scholars, or might be if they agreed with you. The techniques of your discipline are important to essayists, or might be if they studied them. In addition, you have noticed many ancillary benefits. But the one thing you cannot claim is any improvement to your students' work. Would that be a fair assessment?"

And then after a moment: "Why do you think that is?" This is how quickly the cancer spreads. I was curious despite myself.

And like many people in his situation he seemed eager to speak, to take me into his confidence in order to improve his chances. Though perhaps he had been storing up some venom for a long time. "Because it's based on lies! The things we teach people, it's not what we do! No writer in the world takes our advice, or at least no good one. Plot, idea, character, tone, voice, setting, description, exposition—no one thinks about these things. It is a vocabulary invented by idiots to describe concepts that don't exist. No one has any 'ideas.' And if they do, they're a waste of time. Once you start asking yourself how to do something, you can't do it anymore."

I drew the bookshelf that would have been blocked by his head, if he'd had a head. "I've heard that argument before," I said. "Effects rather than causes." (Like most people in my profession, I have an MFA from an exclusive midwestern university.) "But what does that mean? Everybody understands we're talking about a more organic process than the one these words suggest. And we need some kind of vocabulary. Otherwise we're back in the box with inspiration and the nine muses."

That made him angry. I could tell from the way he lifted up his wrists and spread his fingers, pulling away from the cheap, plastic restraints. If I had been able to do justice to his mouth, I would have described his teeth. I sketched for several minutes before I put the rhetorical knife in, the way we had been taught. I leaned forward across the table, close to his ear. "I guess you're talking about some kind of mystic genius and a process nobody can understand."

He had lapsed in the interim into semiconsciousness, but now he started up. "Does it have to be one thing or the other?" His voice was shrill. "A false vocabulary or else none at all? That's the choice that's got us to accept so many phony languages. Is it a coincidence that this one is so exclusionary? That it supports a reactionary way of writing?"

This surprised me. "So you are willing to admit it was exclusionary."

"How could I not?" Drool came from his mouth, but he could not wipe it away. "The language we have put together, the assumptions we make about what constitutes literature even for college students, the realist and minimalist tradition that comes down from the Iowa School, show don't tell, write what you know, that's the natural language of the American upper-middle class. Because it requires so much unearned and misplaced self-confidence. It's a language they don't have to learn; they speak it already. It's the only skill they actually possess."

I drew the buttons down his chest, each with its four holes, but he wasn't through. "All those early models were reactionary, as it turned out. Supported by the CIA. And it's easy to see why. It is the language of class privilege. White supremacy, even. It can't express itself in any other terms.

"Which is why," he said finally, "we have to come up with something new."

When I say "bookshelf," to describe the space behind his head, I realize I have given the wrong idea. There were no books. A few manila folders. The books had already been removed and destroyed. "Wait," I said. "We're not quite done."

I got him to explain to me how the members of his department had selected students for the introductory writing class. "It was always way overenrolled. A maximum of twelve. Some people applied for it every semester and were turned down six, seven times. You had to submit a writing sample. Right away that favored a type of student, someone who already had a sense of themselves, often, as it turned out, someone who had gone to private school. People from another kind of school, maybe someone who had had an overworked English teacher tell them they might have an aptitude, you could see how they gave up after getting turned down once."

"I see," I said, though that had not been my experience.

"It's as if you had an introductory class in the trombone," he muttered. "And you only let in people who could already play. And you reserved all further instruction for that group until their senior year. And the whole process was designed to winnow people away, until the one or two left standing you could take on as your thesis students, and then bicker with your colleagues about who wins the prize. And pretend not to notice how the stories your students produced, year after year, were similar enough to include in the same bad collection, as if written by the same bad artist whose work—what do you know?—bore a bizarre resemblance to your own. The entire college, obviously, was designed as a machine to reward privilege by disguising it as merit. That's why I'm glad to hear you have dismantled it. But my department was undoubtedly the baldest and least apologetic in the way it functioned."

I pondered this. I myself had been a talented story writer at my own top-ten liberal arts college, and had gone through the introductory and advanced classes in preparation for my thesis, which had received highest honors. "Is it possible that your outsider status as a genre writer has colored your perception? That it has made you bitter?" I asked.

"It is not possible."

He had something loose in his mouth that he couldn't remove, because his hands were fastened down. And I could tell he knew he was in trouble. He could see now that we were at odds, because merit has to be the stone foundation of the new society. Everyone in his situation was to be given a score, and so far he was on the cusp—he must have sensed it. Perhaps he had tried to pander, earlier, to what he imagined was my prejudice. But human beings must be measured and judged and held accountable. I stood up and left the room, abandoning him to others as I had my lunch, a cucumber sandwich cut in triangles and a refreshing cup of lemonade.

When I returned for the afternoon session he was more subdued, wet and chattering with cold, the empty bucket tossed into a corner. "So," I said. "If fiction writing is not a collection of skills to be mastered individually and then internalized, how must it be taught?"

The metal table was a high one. Someone had pushed his wheelchair under the rim of it, so that he could lay his cheek down on the surface. Now his voice was muffled and distorted, because he didn't raise his head. His new position had ruined my sketch, though in the margin I was able to create a swift rendering of the slope of his back.

"We need a new vocabulary," I think he said. It was hard to tell. He had developed a little quiver in his foot, which I could see under the table close to my own.

Occasionally I would call in one of my colleagues to wake him. And over the next few hours he offered up a series of ideas about a new course of study. My job is to summarize it and edit it for clarity, and not to pass judgment. My personal opinion, though, is that we must identify talent and separate it out.

As if reading my mind, he said: "The system . . . we'd developed . . . had become . . . frustrating. The students sat in little circles and discussed their finished work as if they already knew what they were doing. Their parents' divorce, reassessing their sexuality—all that is fine material, though you get tired of it. The problems of rich white college students. Anything else, what did they know? Could they help a Nigerian student writing about her visit home? Could they help with a story about pirates, or asteroid explosions, or digital florescent number-change?"

"What would you suggest?" I repeated, irritated in my turn. I am neither white nor rich, but he is, or was. And the last three subjects he mentioned held no charm for me. And the condescending way he talked about his students, I wondered if the choice were privilege disguised as merit, or else privilege undisguised.

I stood up, and took matters into my own hands. After another bout with the bucket he was less combative. I mopped the floor while he shivered and slept. Finally he spoke to me, and I would have had to have been a fool (and not worthy of my MFA and four years of subsequent adjunct work, sleeping in my car, selling blood, and eating at food banks) to take him seriously or at face value. It was my minor in psychology from Haverford that enabled me to understand how his curricular recommendations, when he made them, could be read as a response to his current circumstances, occurring in an alternate reality, say—to use his lingo—where we had more and different resources and a different sense of time and scale. A world or universe where people like himself were lionized and respected and not thrown away like garbage. "I imagine a stone courtyard and an empty fountain," he said, "surrounded by dry, raked gravel and a few stone benches. A warm, dusty wind would shake the lime trees. This is what we learn: music theory, chess, and go. In the breaks, the students make jigsaw puzzles with some pieces missing, the more the better. A student, blindfolded, is led through the world. There are sequences of focused observation. There are classes in drawing, acting, and scenic design. We would alternate periods of extreme attention with extreme inattention, like running mental sprints. We would write no stories at all until the seventh year. Instead, we would tell jokes and invent stand-up routines. We would train ourselves as architects and chefs. This would all be the foundation for a new kind of literature that would have no connection to our actual experience, to what we thought or felt or could imagine. Who has time for any of that anyway? That's not what fiction is about. In our liberation, we could imagine stories in which each word was unique, untethered to consensus meaning. "Ack, ack, ack, ack," we will say. "The plenipotentiary cannot but suffer from the rift."

At other times he would be more subdued. "The only possible story is this one," he said. "A man sits in a room, his chair moving back and forth. It is a flimsy object that he cannot quit. Another man alternately draws and scribbles on an oblong piece of serviceable green plastic with a rubber back. He describes someone without a head. But he can only guess at what he cannot see, the part of the wall and empty bookcase that is hidden behind the actual head in front of him, which consists of two layers of solid yet insulated bone, still largely intact. Therefore he cannot see the crack or rift in the old-fashioned plaster, and the light beyond it that penetrates into the room. You would think he might guess there is a hole, or at least something he has not understood or accounted for, because of the indirect effect of the light, which is not harsh or inefficient like the single tungsten bulb that hangs from the center of the room, but is instead palliative.

"Beyond the head, between two shelves, there is the inside wall of plaster, and an insulated space behind the lath, and then an outside wall. That wall is also breached, and the source of light is out there somewhere, dredged in fog. Way off in the distance, though, lies another country, and a city built entirely of words."

Climate Change

WHAT SEVENTY-YEAR-OLD MAN WOULD not want to receive, on cream-colored stationery, in rigorous yet graceful handwriting, the following instructions?

> Join me on the island, from January fourth to January fourteenth, for a confidential reading of the cards. I've booked us at La Reine Hortense (it still exists!), for the white cabin. Please bring your cock, if you can, as I shall need the loan of it, about three yards at appointed intervals.

Which is how she'd used to talk in the old days. After breakfast, lying on her stomach by the edge of the sea, flies buzzing: "I shall need some cock in a bit. Did you remember to pack it along?"

Barbara had brought in the embossed envelope and of course she was curious. One gets so few actual letters nowadays. "It's about Charles's reading," Mark said, apologetically, because she hated Charles.

"Why is it from London?"

Mark shrugged. "He lives there now, part of the year. But the event is going to be in Philadelphia."

Three yards was really a lot these days, depending on how you measured. A year's supply, maybe more. Later, in the afternoon, he and Barbara sat at the kitchen table. This was in the Hoboken apartment on the third floor. Light fell in strips through the windows over the street. "I'm thinking of doing a follow-up for that old article," he said. "You know the one?"

It didn't take much for her to look at him like that. At fifty-nine she was still beautiful, prettier than Jane had ever been. Dark hair, possibly dyed—who knows these things? She was worried about him, and he was glad for her concern. She was the one who had suggested he might take a trip just by himself. Prior to their marriage he had gone all over. And he had actually written a travel article about Melanesia in the mid-1990s. "I'm interested to see what's happened now," he said, "with climate change."

"It's a long way," she said, scratching the back of her hand. He loved her thick-knuckled fingers. She could do a lot of things, draw, paint, sew. Making things with her hands constituted her own therapy, she claimed. Many things owed her their existence in the world—these napkins, for example, and these napkin rings, carved in the shapes of birds. These cups with the temuco glaze. These framed pictures of the children. This watercolor of laundry on the line.

Because she had so intimately designed the sets and stages, it was easy for him to imagine, late at night in the apartment, that he was wandering around the theater and the green room after a performance. The children had relocated to the West

Coast. They were older than Jane had been when she'd first spoken to him on the plane from Noumea to the island, thirty years before.

"I was thinking somewhere in the next months," he said.

He had been younger too, of course. He had no sense of that. But he saw her clear as a photograph as she'd appeared that afternoon. It was impossible to imagine what she might look like now, and he didn't try.

"Melanesia."

"Yes."

He didn't look at Barbara as she poured tea. Instead he looked at Jane standing in the doorway of the airplane at the top of the ramp, the liquid sun behind her, backpack slung over one shoulder. It was not a romantic moment. The light was so bright. Mark had thought he'd have the cabin to himself. He had found the twenty-seat puddle jumper on the sweating asphalt and had climbed aboard.

She sat down next to him across the aisle. Early in the flight, maybe so he wouldn't get the wrong idea, she announced that she lived in a planned community in Nottinghamshire, a farm without male animals, a village without male inhabitants. It sounded like a location in a fairy story or a utopian fantasy. Women had daughters but no sons, she claimed, and smiled. He smiled back unsurprised—she wore a brownish greenish sleeveless singlet with no bra, and some kind of iron talisman on a cord around her neck. Later he would get to know it well, a pendant in the shape of a hammer. She was squarish, small, with small breasts, short hair with a single braided rat tail. Her arms and shoulders were sweaty. That was the first thing he had liked.

After twenty minutes they circled the volcano and came down onto the island. The pilot opened the door and then went back into the cockpit. Mark got his bag and the two of them descended into the light. The propellers never stopped spinning. The plane moved away as they were walking to the only airport structure, a prefabricated cabin that was deserted also.

"How odd," Jane said. She sounded posh to him. He couldn't remember if he'd thought so at the time. Now, in Hoboken, he heard her voice, filtered, perhaps, though layers of Sunday-night television. By contrast, each visual image was single and precise. At this moment he saw, for example, the tattoo of the quill pen and inkstand on the inside of her forearm and the drop of crimson ink in the middle of her wrist as she brought the back of her hand up to her forehead. In those days it was rare to see such a beautiful tattoo. "My girlfriend made it for me," she'd told him, then or later.

And of course, it was at that moment that he realized he had seen her before, which explained why she had been so chatty on the plane and was walking with him now as if she knew him. That splotch of red. On the boat to Koh Samui. She had been standing by the rail and he had looked at her and her tattoo, and she had turned and stared back, unblinking, which was something a child might do, but not a young woman on holiday. He'd noticed her mouth, which was wide and big.

If he had been able to categorize that realization on the tarmac as they walked away from the moving plane, the red splotch would have signified the first instance of those lapses of cognition that increasingly beset him now, thirty years on, and which he hid from Barbara as much as he could.

At the afternoon tea table she picked up a magazine. But Mark was living in a world where she did not yet exist to him. He stood with Jane on the gravel road, curious to see what happened next. No cars, no houses once they'd left the airfield, but just the dense semi-tropical green, a barricade of vegetation on both sides of the road. Jane looked up at the high cinder cone with its witch's cap of black and gray. "How odd," she said again, and then was silent, because a bus turned at the end of the long straightaway and trundled toward them out of the distance and pulled up opposite, a yellow school bus driven by an obese Melanesian driver who cranked open the doors and motioned them inside. Once again they were the only passengers. Mark wore a T-shirt, cargo shorts, and tire-bottomed sandals. He carried a canvas bag (a change of clothes and his notebooks) and slung it across his lap as he sat down.

Jane, her soft face in profile against the green window, a smudge of dirt above her eye. Jane, uncertain, glancing side-ways toward him—he had read in the Lonely Planet guide-book about a place to stay, a collection of whitewashed huts above a sugar-sand beach. There wasn't another car on the road and they passed nobody on foot. In time the driver pulled over and pointed wordlessly up a footpath leading away from the main road; Mark had told him where they were going in his uninspired French.

"When would you go?" Barbara asked, not that day at the tea table but the next, when they went out to breakfast at a little place on Washington Street and Tenth. Once again he found himself staring at her veined and knotted hands, today in fingerless alpaca gloves, which she now removed.

"I'd have to wait until I could get some time off," he said. "Maybe in January? After Christmas, in any case. I'd see when I could take some time after Christmas. Summertime there, of course."

Mark ran auctions and wrote articles about third-world handicrafts for an online retailer. Christmas was the busy season and then business fell off a cliff. His employers were imbeciles.

But in the 1990s he had written some travel articles for major publications. The one on the South Seas had run in *National Geographic*. It would have been ridiculous to think that Jane had been responsible for that success. But he thought a lot of untrue things, more and more. "I've been looking at pictures of the rising seawater," he said. "Places I've been."

They had arrived on Christmas Eve. At La Reine Hortense, they found the paillote empty, the plein-air central kitchen under its thatched roof. No one in the whitewashed little cabins with their diamond-paned windows. Jane left her backpack propped against a palm tree, and because it was a hot day and it hadn't yet rained, they climbed down through a fringe of vegetation to the beach itself and changed into their bathing suits. Jane turned her back and stripped. She had another tattoo on her side, words of a text. Mark was shyer and changed behind a tree. It was the solitude that made the space so intimate, though the beach was a mile long. White sand, transparent water, high flat-bottomed clouds.

In the Hoboken restaurant he stared down at his eggs, choosing his words. "I went to this place," he said. "This was a year or so before we met. A resort in New Caledonia, just a few cabins by a pretty little beach. Now you look at it on Google Earth, it's almost disappeared," he said, which wasn't true. Only about half of it was gone.

Barbara smiled. "Was there a woman involved? I feel sure there was a woman."

"No, not really. There was one other guest. But she was philosophically opposed to men."

He was about to say she was English until he remembered the cream-colored envelope. "She was from Arizona," he continued. "Plus, she was a lot younger, so it didn't count."

"Huh. I've heard that can be a turn-off," Barbara said.

She was teasing him. As an exercise, he closed his eyes and tried to picture what she was wearing now, right now, sitting across from him. Something brown? Not long before, he had spent an evening with a good friend whose daughter the children had grown up with. He had known her since she was a baby. What was her name? Where had she gone to school?

"Are you okay?" Barbara asked.

"Yes. Fine." He was glad they weren't talking about Jane anymore. He had no desire to share the thought of her, to release her into his wife's custody even in this deceptive version. He paid at the register and they went out into the November morning. Barbara never forgot anything. She wore a brown cardigan with buttons made of bone. Gray piping on the sleeves. He had seen it before, many times.

The thing is, we skate over a plain of ice. If we were to break through into the actual world, we would freeze or drown. Outside in the street, Mark felt on his cheeks a spray of rain just hovering on the edge of snow—cold weather in New Jersey and not even December. All morning he had been thinking about the island, which after all existed now and not just in the past. Jane's letter had reminded him of this. "Now," of course, meant fifteen hours ahead, the middle of the night, and Jane standing naked in the open doorway as the rain came down, the wind in the high palms, Jane simultaneously twenty-one and fifty-one, according to his bewildered arithmetic. Barbara was the only woman he had ever met who never got any older.

No, the island would still exist in January if he managed to get away with this pathetic scheme. Nor was it impossible to imagine that something solid could come out of it, some piece of publishable writing. Already the merging of the past, the present, and the future into superimposed transparencies had given him a sense of vertigo that rendered him unsteady on the broken sidewalk. Barbara clutched his arm.

The thing was, Jane lived inside these merging chronologies; she felt comfortable in them; she searched them out. She was a vocal lover, and not because she yelled and screamed, but because the physical act was always part of a narrative. When she got going, the story would separate into three strands that she would braid together alternately or else murmur to him all together in a fashion that, he thought, would have been unintelligible to someone who was not caught up with her inside the moment, balanced, as she liked to put it, on the edge of the blade.

So for example (and this is what Mark was thinking as he shuffled up the icy sidewalk in the swirling snow, Barbara holding him above the elbow), she could put down a base story in the past tense that typically wouldn't even be about the sex, and it would have a plot—they would be running through the dark woods, something would be chasing them, and it probably would have made sense to separate, only they didn't and instead ended up holding hands beside a river choked with ice.

And also she'd be right there with him in the white room on the island, slippery with sweat, and describing every little feeling or sensation—he had never been with a woman like that.

And at the same time she'd be telling him about the future, another story about them as they had gotten older, or else far, far forward into another time or space, some irradiated beach at the end of the world where there was nothing left to do but fuck. Often in that future time, in what he regarded as the ultimate tour de force, she would look backward through the years they had spent together, many years sometimes, and go back and back until she found the present moment once again, when they'd met in New Caledonia, right now, in fact—only she pretended to misremember what had happened, what was happening. Or she would get the gist but some of the details wrong, like what she was wearing right now, or how she was touching him. Sometimes the future story would be more complicated, a treble melody, because that was another way to think of what she said to him: a Dixieland combination of cornet, trombone, clarinet—present, past, future.

Once she told him, "You saw me on the plane and thought that was the first time. But there was another time you forgot and then remembered, when you saw me on the boat in Koh Samui. And now I'm telling you there was a third time that you haven't remembered even now, when I was waist deep in the water on Langkawi and I called to you to see a baby octopus curled up next to my foot. I was wearing a red T-shirt. How could you not remember? You commented on my tattoo—not that one, no. This one," she said, indicating the line of Hebrew under her arm.

It was possible. People had the same itinerary, the same stops on the same Malaysian Airlines ticket. You ran into them in Penang, Singapore, Papeete. But it was also possible that she was remaking the past for him, extending it in time, a gift of more experiences they'd shared. A little riff on the bass. It was obvious that what was happening here would only last a few days, seven at most, because of the limits of their itinerary.

"What are you thinking about?" said Barbara. They were walking through the snow on Washington Street past the post office. He must have looked worried, because she squeezed his arm. "Just make something up. That's what I need."

She always teased him when she was worried. "I was wondering about Scheherazade in the *Arabian Nights*," he said after a moment. "You always figure she and the king made love every night and then they got up and got dressed, or else half-dressed, and she started talking. But I wonder if it might make more sense if she told him the story while they were actually having sex, part of the act. Depending on the translation, you could recreate what they were doing by paying attention to when the story speeds up or slows down or even parts of the plot."

"Huh."

He wanted her to smile and she did. She let go of his arm and gestured down the street. "Wasn't her younger sister there too? Wasn't she always in there listening? Don't answer that. And don't get any ideas. I guess I should just assume that all these old men walking with their wives are thinking about sex."

Relieved, he shrugged. "You're the therapist," he said, avoiding the word 'shrink,' which she hated. Her profession was a point of fact, though old men were not her specialty. Most of her patients were teenagers. She had a private practice in Ridgefield Park.

It was too hard to explain, but inside he was wondering if Scheherazade had also employed the jazzband method of storytelling, the cornet whispering in the king's ear, the trombone shuddering underneath them all the way back down, and the clarinet twining them in ivied filigree, now and for all future time and future readers. He had to remember thinking about this, so that he could tell Jane about it in two months if he managed to get away. He would write it down when he got home. "Please say 'Scheherazade' when we get back inside," he said, a request he regretted when it still was in his mouth.

"Anything to oblige."

"Unless you forget." He was joking, of course.

"I won't forget." Her lips settled into a line.

There had been a time when he hadn't needed these reminders. He would think about a piece of writing in the middle of the night and in the morning his head would still be full. He remembered the feeling. But now, ideas drifted away. "They flee from me that sometime did me seek," which was a poem he had once thought to be about romantic love. "With naked foot . . ."

On the island, naked or almost naked, sitting cross-legged on the bed, Jane would untie a rayon Indian scarf from around her tarot deck. At least she called it a tarot deck, but the images were not ones Mark had seen before—no fool, no hanged man, no chariot, no tower. She seemed puzzled when he mentioned this. The cards were not mass-produced, she said, but made for her, which was how everything should be. Her girlfriend had painted them. Mark got the impression the girlfriend was a good deal older and held some kind of ceremonial position at the farm.

There were no male figures in this tarot deck. Jane consulted the cards several times a day, shuffling them and then laying them out in various patterns. They influenced her decisions. For example, that was why she and Mark had become lovers in the first place, because of a potential meaning or result. Mark guessed that in Jane's mind at least, she was receiving directions from the maker of the cards. Humbly, he accepted those directions and the limits they imposed, no vaginal intercourse, for example. Sure. Fine. Whatever. In other ways and with other parts of herself she was generous and inventive, and he hoped he was as well.

Actually, it was more as if she had never heard of vaginal intercourse. She looked pensive and doubtful as he tried to explain. Instead, when she brought him to orgasm, often she would pinch the tip of his penis between her finger and thumb so that she could point it away from them when the time came. "Eew," she'd say. Then in a moment she would pat him dry with a washcloth. "Feel better?"

"Much." It was as if his sperm contained some toxic or acidic substance. Her job, as the competent local authority, was to remove the excess and dispose of it responsibly.

"So . . . two sisters in harem pants. Are you thinking about sex?" asked Barbara, now, holding on to his arm amid the blowing snowflakes.

"Poof. You're the one who's obsessed."

The odd thing was: the cards were easy to remember. Even after thirty years he could still picture them, big in her small hands, painted on rough pasteboard perhaps four inches by six. The Cartomancer. The Road. The Golem. The Wind. The Cage. The Prisoner. The Rabbi. The Temple. The Intruders. The Fire Ritual. The Silver Fruit-Tree. The Gift of Happiness. The Cranial Explosion. The House of Healing. The Girl among the Palms. The Musicians. "Take the image," Jane had said once, "and make it three-dimensional. Walk through it or else suspend it in the middle of your mind." At moments over these thirty years he had taken her advice and now he took it again, stumping down Washington Street as if it were The Road, the little shop fronts with the gray-faced women, sinister and haggard under the lowering sky. Up ahead, a bonfire in the middle of the street and a circle of black figures around it, the closest ones rendered in silhouette.

He stepped over the gutter onto the cobblestones. Barbara followed him. But by the time he turned to her, something had happened that had coarsened her face, made her cheeks seem brown and tough as fired clay, her teeth square and yellow in her mouth. He, by contrast, as they stepped forward in the swirling wind, imagined himself losing substance, losing mass until he drifted up into the cold middle air, less a person than a point of view. Down below, clumsy and relentless, Barbara labored up the road past the little shops where the women sold chamomile and verbena and sausages tied up with string. He was down there too, an ambulatory object rather than a man, at least as seen from above, an object with a crest of whitish hair.

On Jane's pasteboard card, the wind consisted of a loose gesture of lines that nevertheless had taken on a human shape whose vagueness made it gender neutral, as Jane herself had grudgingly pointed out. Sketched in ink over a watercolor wash, it had more of an expression than a shape. It knew what Mark did not: where he was going. It saw his peculiar, splay-footed hobble, the way he leaned on Barbara's hand.

Fed with icy boughs, the bonfire smoked and sparked. But the way was blocked with angry women, rich and poor, old and young, gray-haired vagabonds dressed in rags, and schoolgirls in gabardine overcoats and flat brown hats with ribbons at the back. The central gutter was full of frozen refuse. Mark stepped slowly along its rim while Barbara prowled around him in a moving circle, protecting him as she had all their life together. Her yellow eyes gleamed. Her arms and legs pumped rotated and pumped. Hissing and muttering, the women parted to let them through until they reached the bonfire, arranged on a pallet in the icy mud. Beyond it, a cage built of rough saplings, the bark and occasional leaves still affixed, and a middle-aged woman inside, her hair lank and yellow, her homespun shirt ripped down the front. Barbara reached out with her able hands, tightened her grip on two bars of the sapling cage, pulled them apart. The headless, four-sided nails pulled away from the green wood, and the fire hissed and popped, and the circle of women closed in around them, clicking their tongues. When she looked up, Jane's eyes were bleary and red-rimmed, her face smudged with ash. Mark did not recognize her, not yet. At that moment (he saw from above) each one of them had a double nature: Barbara and the golem, Jane young and old, and Mark's body surrounded by its current of air. And the moment itself split and replicated also, containing Mark and Jane on the airplane with the light behind her, and on the island at the instant when, sitting cross-legged, she first looked up at him from the tarot deck, and right now in the cage as she lifted her face, and in the future also, as if he had actually gone back as she'd requested, found a way to disentangle himself in six weeks' time, buy a ticket, get Barbara to drive him to Newark Airport, fly to Sydney and then onward, days of traveling that would culminate at La Reine Hortense, waddling with his suitcase down the road to the paillote and beyond it the white cabin and Jane waiting.

He could see her now, or "now," a middle-aged woman with a round face lined with happiness, which carried inside of it the Jane that she had been. In each of these incarnations he recognized her, something in her, some moment of congress not simultaneously but in a sequence, each cascading into the next like shuffling cards, and resolving here when Jane raised her face to him, her cheeks smudged, her hands raw and bruised as she gripped the sapling bars. The golem had pulled one of them loose, opening a gap. Now, yellow-eyed and fierce, she turned to confront the gathered women, outraged to see a man in their village and outraged also at this interruption of whatever they were doing with their bonfire and their cage and their rabbi—Mark saw her now, erect on the stone steps, dressed in antique ceremonial robes of silk brocade, her arms and hands and face decorated with hierophantic marking. A young woman with her hair bound up, holding in her hands the wands of chaos, the rabbi stood at the temple's brazen door, a seam of light behind her.

"Mark," Jane said, as she had in so many of these moments, as she had when he kissed her that first time after Madame Hortense had blessed their wedding and he had led his bride away from the Christmas fire and the assembled guests, up through the sudden darkness to their cabin above the beach— she had been skeptical at first, uncertain and amused. "Mark, Mark, Mark, Mark," she said, her voice a little breathless in all the gathered moments, the words themselves like cards laid down one after the other.

The water, he knew, would be higher now because of climate change. Perhaps all the white sand beach would be swallowed up. Perhaps even the paillote.

He imagined this would become a ritual every year, now that they had found each other once again. They would return to the island every year until he was very old. Madame Hortense would be glad, her big face split with her red smile. She also, one night after the supper she had made for them— langoustines, some kind of reddish fish—had predicted this, predicted a yearly celebration there—"Oh, but you will see us again. Every Christmas, no?"

"Oui—chaque année—bien sûr. Notre anniversaire."

The rabbi also was dark-skinned, the lines on her face and hands rendered in ochre pigment. Standing above them on the temple steps beyond the cage, she also made prophetic gestures, though of a different sort, minatory, accusing. Mark reached through the gap and took Jane's hand, which was chafed and rough and bleeding from the knuckles. "Mark," she said—it was so good to see her, after thirty years! And yes, he could still perceive the young woman in her body interacting with the younger man inside himself, while at the same time he imagined himself old, older even than now, closing his eyes finally after taking his leave of her. Maybe then also her eyes would be red from crying. Now he pulled her from the cage, and as the rabbi or hierophant took her first step down, and as the golem, eyes brimming with artificial malice, held the crowd at bay, he brought Jane, young and old, into his embrace and kissed her gash of a red mouth.

The doors to the temple slid open, revealing its red interior lit with cauldrons of fire. Raising his head, Mark saw something new in the face of the hierophant, something he did not expect, a tilt of her head, a gesture with her nine-pronged iron staves. The affect of her painted lips was hard to read. With failing strength, he pulled Jane over the wet stones and up the steps. From up above, rising through the cloudy air, he saw a white-haired man, unsteady on his feet, helping or pretending to help a younger woman as the rabbi stood aside to let them pass, and he imagined he heard some shreds of words: "She broke our only law. But there is an extenuating circumstance . . ." The doors opened to admit them while the golem prowled around the bonfire. The temple, or ziggurat, a four-sided pyramid of stepped stone, culminated in a square terrace and a smoking altar, but soon the smoke and mist resolved, and from above he could see the green and silver landscape open up, the wide fields separated by lines of trees. Farther still and he could catch a glimpse of the lozenge shape of Nottinghamshire as if printed in a map, and then more clouds, and he was suffering as the air grew thin. In a moment, as he rose, he knew simultaneously that he was crashing to earth.

***

"They flee from me that sometime did me seek, with naked foot stalking in my chamber. I have seen them . . ." In the white cabin above the beach, among the palm trees, he had told Jane about the things that scared him, the holes in his memory even at forty, the things he already couldn't do anymore.

Late at night, by candlelight, she was laying out his future in the cards. "I think we read that at school." Later: "You know this is . . . unusual, for me." Later: "I'll go up to the temple at the farm when I get back."

"What temple?"

"Of the female divine. That's what we call it. Some of us, anyway."

"Ummm. What's that like?"

"Never you mind. Wouldn't you just like to get your foot inside? I'll tell you, though—it's lovely warm. There's a workshop on the lower level. Everyone as busy as beavers. I could make a figure out of clay, if you'd like, and bake it in the kiln. It will be my gift."

She put her hand on the golem card, which showed a dark figure, back bent, peering at the world through yellow eyes. "But we should know what would be good for you. Straight, probably. Why not? Change is always good."

With her thumbnail, she scratched at the rough pasteboard surface of the card. "Someone with big hands. A healer. You like them dark, don't you? And a bit older than me, I should think, thank you very much indeed. Filthy old man."

Twenty minutes later: "Eew." Ten minutes after that, wind through the mosquito net and the open door. A flicker in the light. Jane sitting against the headboard dressed in underpants and an old T-shirt, the sleeves ripped away. She was working harder now, more methodically, her face almost a parody of concentration. Tongue in the corner of her mouth, at moments, even, as he looked at her. With her thumbnail she had scuffed away a layer in the pigment of the card as if re-inscribing it. She had scraped at some of the background lines, changing the contours of the face and head. "There. You think you might fancy something like that? Take it. My gift to you."

Those words were in his head when he woke up in the hospital out of a light doze. His hand was between Barbara's hands and she was picking at his plastic bracelet. He had slipped and fallen in the street, hit his head, suffered some kind of partial seizure. The doctor would come in to talk about it soon. Bathed in golden light, now Mark lay with the IV in his arm. His skin itched. "Have you told the kids?"

"Not yet. I wanted to be able to say that you'll be fine."

"Am I fine?"

"You'll be fine."

Mark wasn't as sure. Along his elbow and his forearm and his wrist, the skin seemed thin as phyllo dough. By contrast, Barbara looked as good as ever, the planes of her cheeks and nose and forehead, the dark, heavy eyebrows, her expression familiar to him after all these years: imperious, loving, exasperated. "But now they range," he thought, "busily seeking in continual change."

He didn't say it. Barbara said, "Charlie Minter called about the reading. I told him you were too sick. Don't you think that's right? Otherwise I could go with you."

He didn't feel he had to respond. That was the benefit of being sick. "I hate to take away your trip to the South Seas," she said gently. "The island where you met that girl. What was her name?"

He didn't want to tell her, but he did. "Jane," he said. "Jane Gold." It felt like a betrayal. When he closed his eyes, he wondered if he might ever reopen them.

"Rest now," she said, and so he did. But he did not sleep. After some time, he could hear the hospital settling down. From the nurse's station came the sound of distant music on the radio.

They had spent a long time on the beach in their bathing suits. The sand was white, the water clear. When they swam out and looked down, they saw long, striped snakes among the rocks. Later, hungry and thirsty, they came up through the fringe of palms to meet their hosts—they had heard music from the paillote, an old man, as it turned out, playing the horn. This was Georges, and he broke off to greet them and introduce them to Hortense, who was cleaning out the cabins. Other people milled about, drinking wine for Christmas Eve. And Mark could feel there was a misunderstanding right here, one that pleased him, especially since Jane made no effort to correct it—not that she could have easily, because her French was not good. Someone had booked the white cabin, a couple on their "lune de miel." Maybe they wouldn't come. The sun went down, and there was dancing and Christmas music and more wine. Madame Hortense toasted the happy couple. There was something reassuring about the celebration of the group, the gentle teasing about the wedding night; it was cheaper for them to stay in the same room and Jane had no money. They went up to cabin to rinse off and change into clean clothes. "But I'm a bit of a Lesbian, darling," she said.

"I know, I know. Merry Christmas."

"But I'm Jewish, darling." Already they were both a little drunk. The first time they kissed, it was in a crowd of people laughing and clapping and cheering them on. Jane had put on a pale yellow dress and she gave a little curtsy. Later, when night had fallen and he had lit the candle, he looked over and saw her sitting cross-legged on the bed, her dress pulled up. She laid out her cards, placing her forefinger on The Wedding (reversed). "I don't want you getting any ideas about tonight," she said, prematurely. "But it would be fun to come back here when we're old!"

In the hospital, finally, he opened his eyes to the subdued lighting, the dark night outside. He listened as the trumpet came in, bringing with it the melody—a Christmas tune, the first of the season, layered among the other hospital noises. Barbara was on the couch asleep. He admired her for a moment, reaching out his hand. But then he rocked back and forth a bit and managed to slide out of bed, managed to stumble out into the hall, barefoot in his humiliating robe. Everywhere, all around him, people were asleep, lying back on their pillows in the rooms he passed, curled up in the hallways among stacks of towels. He was following the music. And when he reached the nurse's station, a long, high, semicircular desk, he found himself anticipating the clarinet—just a few preliminary notes—waiting for its break. The radio was boxy and old-fashioned, the nurse asleep, her head cradled in her arms. And on the island path from the gravel road down toward the shore, he could see how much had changed, how far the sea had crept up through the palms. Many trees had died and lost their tops. There at the water's edge he caught a glimpse of an old man, turning now to come back toward him the other way.

"Punctuality, Basic Hygiene, Gun Safety"
Paul Park Interviewed by Terry Bisson

You grew up in a college town. Defend.

These decisions about where to be born, where to grow up, one makes them almost arbitrarily, like the character details at the beginning of a story. But they are so hard to correct when things go wrong. I read an article recently by a man who had grown up in a Christian cult and then escaped into academia, only to discover many of the same structures: the abusive hierophants at the top, the un- or undercompensated labor at the bottom, the cruel assumption of superiority based on self-serving definitions of excellence, either spiritual or intellectual. My parents were priests in that cult, and it took me a long time to recognize the insidious ways in which privilege disguises itself as merit, or "merit," among upper-middle-class Americans. On the other hand, it's a lovely little town; I still live there.

Soldiers of Paradise *was your first work. Or was it? Where did you try to place it? How did it end up with Hartwell?*

I wrote a novel before *Soldiers of Paradise* about a murder in a monastery. I was living in New York in the 1970s, working in an advertising agency and hating it. So I quit to work in a squash club and write *Lamb's Blood*, which was never published. *S of P* came later, after two years in Asia. I was less green by that time and knew enough to get an agent, which took a year or so. Adele Leoni agreed to represent it with David in mind. He was with Arbor House then, and I remember the whole process taking about a week. The advance was not large.

Ever spend a winter on Block Island?
I did! Maybe in 1973? My parents had a house by the water, unheated except for a kerosene stove in one room. I ate a lot of Gorton's Codfish Cakes. I read Russian novels, and my dog and I walked all over the island, which was far more rural in those days. It would be easy to plot out a story that would make that winter a pivotal episode in my life, if you liked those sorts of stories.

You sometimes appear in your own stories. Is that by invitation?
I used to think it was a bad and politically retrograde idea to borrow anything from your own experience and put it in your work, except in the most glancing and indirect way. So calling characters "Paul Park" was my little joke. The name always seemed improbable to me, and artificial, since no one used it when I was a child. Once when I was working at Smith/Greenland I put it into a sample advertisement, and the client accepted everything but that detail. They told me, "No one could ever be named 'Paul Park,'" which seemed reassuring and right to me, and I took those words to heart. I had the art director substitute "Frank Masters," which the client liked and I did too, because it is a phrase that means something—I

once had a student named Chace Lyons. Lately, of course, I've found characters more like myself haunting my stories, and I give them all sorts of made-up names.

When did you start fooling around with metafiction? What is metafiction, anyway?

A metafictional story is one that is aware of itself and knows that it is artificial. In most stories you are asked to imagine you are finding out about real people and their problems. So, for example, in this interview the reader might imagine an actual author answering actual questions in a way that suggests what he actually thinks. But what if that becomes increasingly unlikely? What if the response to a question about metafiction appears foolish or fraudulent, in a way that suggests either (a) that the interviewer is manipulating the answers and the author doesn't exist, or (b) that there is no author and no interviewer either, and the whole exchange is being manufactured by some unknown writer for a new purpose. Usually there is a metafictional break in the story, as, for example, here, where the reader understands they're being toyed with. In theory, the whole tone of the interview might change, as every subsequent answer is now suspect.

This way of thinking has always been interesting to me, as it turns out—recently I was cleaning up after a fire and came across some stories I'd written in school. Metafiction. I think it might be because I'm bad at conventional plotting, the straight line between A and B that "takes away all hope," as Grace Paley describes it.

Didn't you write a Dungeons & Dragons novel? How did that come about?

I was in Seattle teaching at Clarion West, and at a party I met one of the editors at Wizards of the Coast, who publish the Forgotten Realms books. My son had started to play the game with a posse of his friends, and I thought it would be fun to write a story for *Dragon* magazine, which I knew he read, and have it show up on his screen. Later, the same editor approached me for a novel, and I accepted under the condition that I could borrow the characters my son and his friends had invented for their game and base the novel under them. And one other condition: I could write it under a pen name, which would then appear in a metafictional novel called *All Those Vanished Engines*, about, among other things, a man named "Paul Park" who writes a Forgotten Realms novel under the same pseudonym and quotes from it inaccurately.

You seem more interested in ceremony than actual behavior. Are you aware of that? Does it worry you?
Is there such a thing as actual behavior, for conscious beings? How would that even work? Isn't everything a performance of itself? When I was living in the Congo, sometimes foreign guests would want to go to so-called tribal villages, where people who make a show of eating their traditional meals, wearing their traditional clothes, pursuing their traditional activities. So: melancholy and pathetic, and only tolerable if you remembered that everything is like that.

Do you ever workshop your own stuff?
No—that would be awful. And what would be the point?

You furnished the soundtrack for a museum installation. How did that come about?

I've done two museum shows, one at the Massachusetts Museum of Contemporary Art and one at CityPlace in West Palm Beach. In both cases I provided the text for a mixed-media sound installation assembled by the artist Stephen Vitiello. Both turned into wonderful collaborations. They were his commissions, but he asked me to be part of the team, because when he accepted the assignment at MASS MoCA, he remembered from one of my author bios that I lived in the same town as the museum, and he asked them to hire me. They were like, "Who?"

Are you a Christian? What's with all the Jesus and Mary books?
I tried to be a Christian for a while, when I was in New York. I loved the smell of the old stone and polished wood. I loved the music. That sounds superficial, but I responded to those things in a way that still seems significant to me. I didn't love trying to convince myself I believed things I actually didn't. I got belief all tangled up with faith. Nobody really believes anything, it turns out. The books came later and are unrelated. At least I think they are.

Your father was a physicist, at Princeton for a while. Ever meet Einstein?
Yes, my father was at the Institute for Advanced Study in the early 1950s. He knew all those guys: Robert Oppenheimer, Richard Feynman. Not well, I think. Freeman Dyson was the only one who became a family friend. Once my father introduced my mother to Albert Einstein at a party. "I was expecting someone so much taller," she said. Later she suggested he might not have not found that funny.

One sentence on each, please: Carol Emshwiller, Mick Jagger, Ludwig Wittgenstein.
Carol Emshwiller is the only great writer whose smile can light up all of lower Manhattan. I regret pretending, when Mick Jagger checked into the racquet club where I was working, that I didn't recognize him and indeed had never heard of him, which was a pointless and pathetic lie. Despite quoting him once in a short story, I have never read a word of Ludwig Wittgenstein and never will.

Favorite whiskey?
Whisky, please: Laphroaig (Islay). For blended whisky (stirred, really): Ye Olde Earl (Edinburgh, London, Kathmandu).

You once brought me a bottle of Ye Olde Earl. Fortunately, it was tiny. You have taught writing at Clarion and several colleges. Ever have a real job?
No, I don't think so. I worked for the City Council in New York. I worked in advertising and in health clubs. I was a janitor. I worked in retail and sold Chinese antiques. I wrote catalog copy and artists' profiles. Now I'm a college professor. Real jobs are as chimerical as real Americans.

Do your students ever actually read SF? Do you have two or three things in particular you teach? Any things you have to unteach?
No. They used to have read Orson Scott Card but not anymore. I teach a number of different kinds of writing: Utopian Fiction, Imitations and Parodies, Science Fiction of the African Diaspora, Expository Writing for Art Historians, as well as Creative Writing. My college is generous that way, possibly

because, to put it mildly, I lack formal credentials. I try to teach (a) punctuality, (b) basic hygiene, and (c) gun safety. I try to unteach Raymond Carver, show don't tell, and write what you know.

What was your first literature? Were you ever a reader of SF or Fantasy?
I read myths and fairy tales, Arthurian legends, Tolkien, and Le Guin. I never read any comics or hard SF. I wish I had. It's too late now.

You were friends with James Sallis in New Orleans, and now with John Crowley in New England. So tell me, why is it that some major, even celebrated, writers, given the opportunity to jump ship from genre, don't?
I think it turns out to be hard. When I tried to strike away with the Jesus books, *The Gospel of Corax* and *Three Marys*, David Hartwell told me it was never going to work, that I'd never climb out of the box. He turned out to be right. The stain of genre doesn't necessarily affect the work, but it affects the perception and reception.

How come you haven't won any major awards? All your friends have.
It's true. Every single one of them. And not just participation trophies, either, but major, national awards. They put them up on the mantelpiece and dust or polish them. They survey them with quiet pride. Sometimes they stroke them with anxious, feverish fingers, I hear. By contrast I am forever denied that experience. That glass case is closed to me. And yet . . .

Do you have a regular drill for writing? You know what I mean.
Nope. Not anymore. When I was living by myself, my routine was to piss and moan for a solid year until I had built up enough panic and distress, then pound out a book in a few months. That system turned out to be unconducive to domestic life and fatherhood. When the kids were young, I developed a more disciplined schedule and got up every morning at four so I could write before they woke up for school. Now they're gone, and I'm sorely in need of a new way.

You sort of slip and slide among genres. Do you use them as fences or chutes?
I never developed the hook of self-imitation, from which commercial success so largely depends. Do you think Jasper Johns *wanted* to paint all those flags and stars? This is especially true in genre, where one is rarely rewarded for change. I think it has helped me to never have made much money. If the Princess of Roumania books had been a great success, I could imagine sitting around thinking, "So, what about Bulgaria? Moldova? Transnistria?"

What's your position on the big bang? Evolution? Are you aware that they are just theories?
It's hard for me to believe in things I can't visualize—I mean actually believe in them and not just be comfortable saying so. The big bang theory sounds more like a religious moment than a scientific one, possibly because it seems so *fiat lux*. As for evolution, I don't dispute the facts of the case, just the theorizing that rise out of them, which seems to me reductive and depressing. In general, I have no interest in abstract thought.

Your wife is a theater professional. Ever write a play or a screenplay?
No, but I've thought about it. I'm not alone in this, I hear.
Three Marys would make a good play.

When you were a kid, did everyone call you Pogo or just your mean sisters?
That particular cognomen, from the great Walt Kelly comic strip, started with my parents, who disliked the actual name they'd given me. Everybody called me that except in the most formal situations. And I don't think they were being mean . . . except, wait a second now. Wait just a gosh darn minute. "Dagnabbit," as Pogo might say.

The Gospel of Corax *about the "lost years" of Jesus was based on what?*
I was going on a hiking trip to the Garhwal Himal and had a few hours to kill while the Indian consulate processed my visa. So I walked over to St. Bartholomew's on 51st Street and Park Avenue, which is a beautiful neo-Byzantine pile. I sat in a side chapel, and the whole shape of the novel fell in my lap all at once: Jesus' trip to India. I had been primed for thinking about it for some years, ever since the time I'd spent in Rajasthan and Uttar Pradesh years before. I had gotten interested in theosophy because of all the references to it in Indian cities, roads named after Annie Besant or Madame Blavatsky. And it was commonplace in famous temples to hear people tell you Jesus of Nazareth had worshipped there. I was aware of the theosophist legend that Jesus had lived and studied, and even died, at Hemis Gompa in Ladakh—my great-grandmother had run a theosophical society in New Haven. There I was in St.

Bartholomew's. Old stone, polished wood, half-heard music from the nave. It was as if the book was already in my hand.

You were part of the Mount Thoreau expedition in 2015. Are you an admirer of Thoreau or do you just follow Stan Robinson and Gary Snyder around?

The latter, sadly. I like to read people only after I climb the mountain named after them. It gives me a better sense of what they're like, what to expect. *Walden* had always seemed a bit hectoring to me. But I'd loved *The Maine Woods* and wrote about it for Laurie Glover's anthology. Step by measured step, until the man is way off the deep end.

What poets do you read for fun? Ever read mysteries? Why not?

I disapprove of mysteries. I'm not sure why. Disapproval is like that, for me. It comes from a place of stupidity. I imagine them as over-determined and controlled, and I don't care to be told differently. Poets? I read a lot of poets. Right now today? Ocean Vuong and Celia Dropkin.

My Jeopardy *question. I provide the answer, you provide the question. Answer: A boathouse on an undiscovered bay.*

What is a fine and narrow cylinder of neglect?

You were one of the first to buy a Saturn, yet you rarely write about space travel. Explain.

Why write about it when you can live it? Those early models, I remember, when the company was still independent—downshifting into ninth gear on a summer night, at the old abandoned wooden ski ramp near my house, you could break out of the troposphere at an incline of sixty degrees, and she'd stop shuddering and shaking, and spilling all the coffee in your lap. Such bliss to hit that cold still quiet place. One tank of gas—Jesus. Past the Kuiper Belt, you could wrap up in a sleeping bag and coast. And in those early days they had refueling stations along the way.

If you could low-orbit any planet or satellite in the solar system for several hours, which would it be?
Haven't you been listening?

You were spotted at Everest Base Camp some years ago. What were you doing, collecting empties?
Yes, the place is a trash heap. I prefer the corpses higher up. The things people leave, they should take away. The things they take away, they should leave. Go figure.

So what's next?
I've been working on short fiction, mostly, for the past few years. And a novella called *Lost Colonies of the Ancient World*. It might be that I never finish it. Maybe it's important always to be working on something that defeats you. And I've been researching a new historical novel set in Roman Gaul. "Vercingetorix" is a name that holds, in my opinion, irresistible and universal appeal. I've been rolling it around my mouth since I was a child.

A Resistance to Theory

SHE STOOD OUTSIDE THE lecture hall examining the poster. The image was murky, perhaps a tattooed human face, perhaps a tribal mask. Under the title of the talk, Professor Farinelli had included this bio in small print:

> My writing has focused on developing a critical theory that would support an ethnography of the postanthropologic otherwise. My recent work examines the hegemony of the predeceased in late liberal settler colonies from the perspective of the politics of embodiment, eroticism, and narrative form. My ethnographic analysis is illuminated by a critical assignation with the traditions of American pragmatism and continental theories of immanence and intimacy.

Seldom had Yvette felt such excitement. And yet her hands did not shake. It had been raining outside the library, a cold November drizzle. Momentarily she laid her right palm against the polished surface of the wall, and laid her forehead there too. She caught a glimpse of a blurry reflection before she turned away. "Immanence," she whispered. "Eminence. Imminence." The words themselves were interchangeable, designed for a purpose not limited to comprehension. Even she, defeated as she'd been by stuff like this, could see the beauty of that purpose if you let your mind go.

Crowell Concert Hall, 4 p.m., November 19th—here she was. The text promised a manifestation of great power. She could only hope she'd come prepared. Combing her left hand through her wet, stringy hair, she pulled open the double doors and took her seat.

Yvette knew she would have to be careful. She had purposely come late. She had already achieved a limited celebrity because of the disruptions she had caused, not here, but in colleges and lectures elsewhere on the East Coast. Once she had taken the train down from Boston to New York, hoping to confront Slavoj Žižek, the Slovenian cultural theorist, in the quadrangle at Columbia University, to express her admiration or else maybe kill him. But at the last moment she had paused, irresolute, struck dumb by what he'd said about false consciousness.

It wasn't so easy, distinguishing the postanthropologic from the predeceased. Sometimes the evidence was mixed. Now she unbuttoned her raincoat in the cavernous uncrowded room. She had chosen a seat near the back next to the aisle, in case she had to escape. Attempting to project a sense of confidence, she spread her knees apart while she examined the bald head of the man in front of her. She could hear the speaker at the podium below her in the stepped well. Momentarily she closed her eyes, not yet ready to look. In preparation, she listened only to the sound of Professor Farinelli's voice, seductive and low. She did not listen to the words, not yet. Instead, and in order to provide a sense of contrast, she found herself remembering one of her favorite quotations from Judith Butler, a printed text, as it happened, which she now recomposed in a separate mental theater, analogous to this one:

> . . . Gay identities work neither to copy nor to emulate heterosexuality, but rather, to expose heterosexuality as an incessant and *panicked* imitation of its own naturalized idealization. That heterosexuality is always in the act of elaborating itself is evidence that it is perpetually at risk, that is, that it "knows" its own possibility of becoming undone . . .

Lately, this passage had become her rubric, her touchstone, her flaming sword to separate the false from the true. How beautiful it had appeared to her the first time she had read it, sitting by herself in Mugar Library! Each word was like a boat slipping gradually from shore, now caught in the current, now away. How lovely to see those painters broken, first to relentless denotation, and then—the restraint subtler and softer, but for that reason more oppressive—to connotation also; the ropes strain one by one, and then they snap. Geniuses like Butler—living, breathing women—had created a whole language of experience that drifted alongside us without touching us at any point. ". . . Gender is a kind of imitation for which there is no original . . ."—not just gender, but language also worked that way.

Yvette opened her eyes. She glanced at her confederate on the other side of the hall, a man close to her own age or a little younger. He lolled back in his seat, his left foot, shod in a heavy boot, twitching on the dark carpet. Like her, he wore a long raincoat. He smiled or grimaced, it was hard to tell.

She'd contacted him on Craigslist when she was still in Boston and then met him at a coffee shop called Klekolo, on Court Street. They'd barely said two words. Then he'd preceded her up the hill. Less of a celebrity, he'd been here from the beginning.

He smiled or grimaced and then turned his head. At the wooden podium perhaps sixty feet away, Professor Farinelli paused in mid-phrase, a pen or a pencil in her right hand. Yvette had looked her up on the Wesleyan website and had been grimly unsurprised to see there was no photograph. Now she assembled her impression: red fingernails, red lipstick, the ghost of a smile—a pretty woman with shining copper hair and pale skin, so very pale. Yvette felt a tingling sensation along her scalp. The trick was to spot the fakes, the imitations, the weeds that grew among the flowers, searching for safety from the gardener.

Farinelli was one of the weeds. She would have to be up-rooted before she and her kind had choked the entire bed, the entire field. Yvette had been sure walking in. Now she was doubly sure.

Yvette was a graduate student at BU. Her thesis advisor in the months before her death had trained her in the tiny differ-ences between the Butlers and Kristevas of the world, say, and these bitter simulations. She held clutched in her left hand the program for the conference, sodden from the rain. It contained the description that had seduced her here, in a car this time, from her empty Somerville apartment:

Is the posthuman a further evolution of humanity, or have human beings always been posthuman? If so, as evidence increasingly suggests, in what sense? What are the implications of gender, race, class, and sex, among other categories, for the new, embodied constitution of posthumanity? And in both practical and political terms, what is the essential difference between the posthuman, the transhuman, the anti-human, and the cyborg?

Food for thought. How insidious, how vicious, was Farinelli's use of the word "evidence"! And now this, from her pretty, lipsticked mouth, as she achieved the peroration of her introductory address: "The difficulty of life's embodiment as a possible interpolation between disciplinary discourse and actual political practice offers itself as a matter of strident urgency. What this conference aims to advance, however, is neither a notion of life already encapsulated in its dense social network nor life as an established, already articulated political manifestation. We are attracted by life as such, caught in a more basic network of ganglia and capillaries, and brought thereby to its radical existence and pure is-ness, one that permeates, challenges, and ultimately escapes the hegemonic order that strives to embody it. Yet our attraction feeds on and desires to control much wider debates. Recent work has already begun to interrogate the limits of biology, posing a series of questions regarding the distinctness of natural life over artificially created life or even so-called death. Especially after I emphatically discard any claims to the superiority of the first of these overlapping states, what follows is a return to life's pure potentiality and its political implications either as material or immaterial presence, or animate or inanimate force."

Yvette found herself staring at the speaker's mouth, the bruised, pillowy lips, the clever teeth. "Oh, I've got you," she murmured to herself. "I've got you."

Reflexively she took her pulse, a habit she had gotten into. Then she reached into the inside pocket of her raincoat where she kept Professor Larsen's stiletto. Always at these moments of decision, she imagined herself balanced as if upon a granite ridge, high in the air under a harsh yet forgiving sun, an abyss of formlessness on either side. Propelled in her choices by those soft, insistent rays, nevertheless she felt a moment of relaxation, perhaps the only moment in this entire anxious week. Almost without paying attention, she found herself aware of the young man sitting beside her, a student, she guessed, one of the few in the hall. Most of the attendees were at least in their thirties, and she saw a number of gray heads. This one—dark hair, glasses—was cute in a nerdy way, and she appreciated the intensity with which he listened to this fiend from the frozen pit of hell. As always with her kind, Farinelli was speaking in a kind of code, which meant one thing to her minions and something else to stooges like this boy, desperate for understanding and vulnerable for that reason.

". . . The embodiment of life sets up each confrontation as a unique case in our hopeless attempt to reach justice. This afternoon I've tried to excavate the aesthetic politics of life and death as a methodological intervention into the apparatuses and possibilities of nonhegemonic practice. In addition, I've tried to suggest how violence and control produce aspects of resistance, located in our individual reactions to the powers reshaping the living world. I've tried to isolate some safe-holds that the diverse forms of posthumanity will occupy to flourish and survive, in resistance to the structures and procedures of surveillance and control. Through a discussion of mutual inter-rogation (or indeed, an interrogation of discussion practices), I aim to see a new style of human and posthuman eroticism as integral to a deconstruction of hegemonic power. This new style calls for a dissolution of the subject and the emergence of a hybrid, nonsovereign being. Now let us allow new practices of self-fashioning, self-identification, or else an inner experi-ence of this new eroticism show the way."

By "sovereign," perhaps she meant, in Butler's terms, the incessant and panicked imitation that created the ideal: actual, real things, in other words—for a moment Yvette felt, or imag-ined she felt, the throb of her pulse above the collarbone. From her own safe-hold of relaxation on the granite ridge, the sky above her bright and blue enough to cause her nose to bleed, Yvette saw the speaker glance up toward her. The Q&A was about to start. She groped again for the stiletto.

But what did she imagine she would do with it? Surely to display it would invite a premature dissolution of the subject. Or was it only useful as a source of comfort, a masturbatory practice of self-fashioning, self-identification, or else an inner experience of . . . eroticism? The dialectic was troubling, and now on the high ridge, suddenly she felt the rocks shift un-derfoot. While she was listening she had kept Butler in mind, using her as a model to compare and distinguish the imitation and the true. She had murmured and re-murmured the quota-tion, a revolving and self-sustaining mantra: ". . . a panicked imitation of its own naturalized idealization. That heterosexuality is always in the act of elaborating itself is evidence . . ."

But—evidence, evidence: surely Butler's use of the word "evidence" was as problematical as Farinelli's! Upon first reading, Yvette had found herself obscurely touched, as if evidence could be a type of aspiration. But now, unbalanced over the rock precipice, she felt a vertigo of doubt. Perhaps she had been wrong! From that small crack in the text, new problems now emerged.

Perhaps Farinelli and Butler held other things in common. Yvette's mentor and advisor had once explained to her the difference between profound and superficial truth: We recognize the deepest accuracy of a statement only if its opposite is just as accurate. "Man is born chained," in Professor Larsen's example, "yet everywhere he is now free—just as verifiable, depending on what you think of the umbilical cord." Then she had gone further and reversed the customary valorization: "Profound truth is for suckers, or else people who don't give a damn." Of course she'd been drunk when she said this, and of course she had paid for her insight a week later, alone in a Cleveland hotel room. Cornered by her enemies, she had denied them the satisfaction, finally, of sucking her dry.

But with a sudden lurch of fear, Yvette realized that the Butler quote was also full of profound truth. She'd been fooled—gulled like a rube, as Professor Larsen might have said—by what she'd imagined was its separate language of dissociation, a kind of poetry, she'd thought, like certain stanzas of Bob Dylan, Talking Heads, or John Ashbery. But now, with a fascinated horror, she saw she could negate or contradict each one of Butler's phrases with no loss of meaning . . . That homosexuality is always in the act of elaborating itself is evidence that it is perpetually at risk . . .—even better! The sentence even scanned as if yearning that way.

"I see you are beginning to understand," remarked a soft, supple voice inside her head. Yvette peered backward over her shoulder and observed a shrouded figure at the top of the aisle, now blocking the exit. She scanned the other side and saw other figures massing there. Was it possible she was alone here, alone among the posthuman? The bald man in front of her turned his head, gave her a look—he was much younger than she'd anticipated, or at least he looked younger. There were no lenses in his wire spectacles. Elsewhere she saw the gray heads turn to look at her, revealing unlined faces, indeterminate ages, feral smiles. And even the fellow from Craigslist, perhaps Farinelli had hired him to tempt Yvette into revealing herself, so that posthumanity might gather her in.

She refused to look at him. Too charitably perhaps, she had imagined a remnant of compassion in the bone-pulverizing density of the lecture segment she'd just heard. She'd imagined an attempt to limit casualties by boring the civilians from the room. Only the lost causes had stayed, the addicted, like this kid on her left hand, nervous, raising his finger. He wanted to ask a question. "Don't expose yourself," she murmured.

Then she rose from her seat, pushed back her still-wet hair. If this conference had been designed to lure her and exclude everyone else—or almost everybody—because of the concrete difficulties of its subject matter, then she would give them a show. If she were alone in this room—or almost alone—then she would demonstrate the superiority of natural life to the last of her ability, to the end. She would demonstrate the power of the real. And she would protect this addled student. "Put your hand down," she told him. "For God's sake put it down."

All eyes were upon her, even her own eyes, from the high stone ridge where she looked down. She saw as they did a dark-haired woman, untall, unthin, unlovely, naturally superior, perhaps, but in no other way. She reached into the breast pocket of her raincoat and heard a suppressed hiss from the bald man looking up at her from the seat in front. But she removed a pocket handkerchief and used it to blot her cheeks. As she'd suspected, her mascara had dissolved a bit—she'd seen it from above. She blotted her lips, now, too. "Thank you for a very interesting talk," she said, replacing the handkerchief in another pocket. "I couldn't help thinking, as you spoke, of what Butler says about performativity. I wonder if you'd care to comment on how the act of being human might also be considered performative, as she says, a kind of imitation for which there is no original, and which produces the notion of the original as a consequence of the imitation. Do you think that's so? By contrast, you could also argue that these other types you mention, posthuman, transhuman, antihuman, have no significance except as imitations of ordinary human beings. In which case—imitations of imitations—what is their ontological status? I omit cyborgs from my consideration because, as specifically technological hybrids, they seem to me to be in a different category. Even as metaphors, they represent a weakness in the entire conceptual framework of this conference . . ."

"Fuck me," groaned the Craigslist man. "You don't even want to know about their goddamned cyborgs. Metaphors— shit," he said, kicking his leg even farther out into the aisle, freeing the holster strapped to his right thigh, now for a fraction of a moment visible in the vent of his coat.

So he was on her side, after all! No doubt it was the purest hubris (against which her advisor had persistently warned her) for Yvette to have imagined that all this—the posters, the conference—had been conceived and designed just to lure her . . .

Her nonquestion dwindled to a close. At the bottom of the hall, Farinelli made a gesture with her pen. "It is interesting that you should mention," she began, while at the same time the soft voice inside Yvette's throbbing skull provided subtext: "You little piece of shit . . ."

She didn't have to turn her head to imagine the tall figure at the top of the aisle pulling the scarf from her face. She didn't have to imagine the handsome, potentially transhuman features of Judith Butler, the Maxine Eliot Professor of Rhetoric at Berkeley. Feeling stronger now, buttressed by the presence, perhaps, of others like her in the hall, she spoke up again: "As some of you may know, I am writing my dissertation on Kristeva's theory of abjection . . ."

She listened to another deflating hiss from the bald man in front of her. She studied his mouth, his perfect teeth. Again she felt a sudden vertigo. Was it also hubris for her to imagine, on the other side of the hall, at the top of the other aisle a second figure pull the shawl from her face to reveal the ageless, pallid flesh of the distinguished Franco-Bulgarian philosopher that she had named? She didn't glance that way. Instead she spouted some contemptuous nonsense that conflated the pre- and post-avant-garde, not even bothering to make sense. Two could play at that game. Actually, any number could play.

But as she spoke, she listened to the voice inside her head, as insidious as if it were her own chafing conscience or self-doubt. "Ah, yes, I am aware of you. I can feel your heart knocking in your chest, the blood pulsing at your temples. I was the keynote speaker at the Cleveland symposium. And I was with your dissertation advisor at the last, Larsen—that was her name. A second-rate scholar, I'm afraid. I had not seen so much blood."

"Enough," said the speaker at the podium. She dropped her pen, and it rolled a little way across the floor. She made a fist of her left hand, drawing the red nails inward. "Ms. Daume," she continued, "we are all aware of how difficult it has been for you since Karen Larsen's death. Believe me, you were not the only one of us affected—always it is a terrible thing, when a mentor and a friend decides to end her own life. That does not give you the right to . . ."

Someone had come down the aisle from the top of the hall and now stood at Yvette's elbow. "Ma'am," he said, a campus policeman, surreptitiously summoned, perhaps, when she'd stood up. She looked behind her, where she had imagined Julia Kristeva at the top of the hall. Another policeman approached from that side; oh, it was true, these philosophers could manifest in many forms. But on the other hand, how foolish now it seemed to her, to think these world-famous scholars might have traveled all this way to lay a trap for her. She had been squeezing the hilt of the stiletto in the inside pocket of her overcoat; now she released it, raised her hands, spread her palms, and allowed campus security to escort her up the stairs, out the double doors, and down into the barren, twilit courtyard. From her high granite ridge, polished smooth by the wind, she looked down on her own bedraggled head, where she stood, a minute later, at the corner of Court Street, in tears.

***

"I'm sorry, ma'am," said one of the policemen, "but you can't stay on campus. If you just go down the hill, you'll find . . ."

"No, I'll go," she said, wiping her nose with her handkerchief. "And thank you, officer. You saved my life back there. I don't know what I might have . . ."

"That's okay. If you just . . . "

It was almost dark when she did find it: a safe-hold, a place of refuge, a coffee shop on Main Street where an hour later she sat clutching the remains of a bran muffin, and reading for the third or fourth time the introduction to Kristeva's *Black Sun: Depression and Melancholia.* But finally the man from Craigslist sauntered by the plate-glass window. He pressed his face against the glass, cupped his hands around his eyes. The rain had stopped. When he saw her, he came inside, took off his coat and hat. "May I?" She saw no sign of his revolver.

"I think I'd rather be alone."

He shrugged, then sat down opposite her at the small, square table. He leaned across it with his elbows on the polyurethaned surface, his long hands near her plate. "That was quite the Q&A," he said. Then he leaned closer: "Listen, I know what you're thinking. You think you're wrong, but you were right. I saw some manifestations, just for a moment. Just before the police showed up."

"Please go away."

He sighed, rubbed his long, crooked nose. "It's humiliating. But there's a chance. You must know who killed your advisor."

Yvette swallowed three times before she spoke. "I did," she confessed. "My dissertation bored her to death. She had a dozen pages with her in the bathroom."

The man smiled. "Always a risk," he said. "But I feel sure that was not the proximate cause. Barely a contributing factor."

"You don't know. You never tried to read it. Besides, the door was locked on the inside. No sign of a . . ."

"Sure. A locked door isn't much of an obstacle to a creature like that."

"And she'd been depressed. Her husband told her he was leaving."

But Yvette knew Karen would have been honored to see Judith Butler through the peephole, let alone Julia Kristeva.

She looked out at the slick sidewalk under the streetlight. "Sure," the man said. "Sure."

He himself looked so mournful, momentarily, that he was almost handsome, big features, small beard, chapped lips. His hands were big, his knuckles prominent. "Look," he said, "I've been mapping out what I call power nodes in the different universities, mostly in the Northeast. The oldest and the wisest ones are territorial. The one I saw, she's not that wise, not in comparison."

"You mean Farinelli."

"No. God, no. Farinelli's just a wannabe, just starting out. Butler's the transhuman here, but I don't think she's made the change to full-fledged antihuman. Not yet. She won't have had the time. She was born in 1919, made, created, you could call it, in the late thirties—maybe by Martin Heidegger, which would explain the anti-Semitism. It would have come in through the blood."

"1919 . . . ?"

"Sure. Hadn't you guessed? It's Paul de Man. We're talking about Paul de Man."

"Judith Butler is Paul de Man?"

He slapped his hand on the table. "That's who you're dealing with here. That's why the imitation is so good. The actual transformation was at Yale in the early eighties. He must have known it was going to come out, the story of his collaboration with the Nazis during the war. He must have taken this young graduate student from Bennington, groomed her, inhabited her body—Jewish, a woman. How he must have laughed! And of course her academic work is all about performativity. Not to mention anti-Zionism."

"But she's at Berkeley," objected Yvette. "Berkeley and Columbia. Farinelli's the one here, isn't she?"

"I'm not sure. I was hoping to find out this afternoon."

She glanced away. "Well, I fixed that," she said.

Depressed and melancholic, she picked up her book. But she had lost the thread. Nor did she care to imagine the long drive home. After several minutes she looked up. The man hadn't gone away. He hadn't even changed the subject. "Why are you reading that posthuman trash?" he said. "I think there's someone else here, someone important. Maybe somebody from Frankfurt. Farinelli seems too raw to me, too young."

Why was he staring? What did he want? She didn't know his name, didn't want to know it. She found herself irritated by his bossiness, his explanations: "What's your field? Are you a poet?"

Startled, he drew back his hand. "Why do you ask?"

She put down the book. "Well, those are the battle lines, aren't they? The Hatfields and McCoys. Plato kicked the poets out. We're losing, in case you hadn't noticed." She had folded into eighths the remains of her muffin's pleated baking slip. Now with her thumbnail she was rubbing it smooth on the surface of the table. "I was hoping you were a poet."

His eyes were quite attractive, kind of a speckled brown. This close, she could see his contact lenses. "I think that's an oversimplification," he said. "Plato was a poet, too. *The Republic* is a piece of poetry."

"Oversimplification is my new crusade. You think our enemies might hate themselves. Good to know. An Achilles heel, not that it gives us an advantage. For Plato, everything's an imitation of the ideal. But does he ever say that's bad? Maybe the imitations are always better, as it turns out."

The man smiled. "He would have disagreed while he was alive. By now I'm sure he's changed his mind. You could ask him. I think he's still at Harvard. Emeritus now, finally."

"Yes," she said, "I'd heard the average age at Harvard for a tenured professor is a hundred and ninety five. A lot of wisdom all around. I didn't know Plato was skewing the numbers."

"It would take more than that," he murmured. Were they flirting? It was hard to tell. She decided to think so. "What are you doing here, really?" she asked. "It wasn't to see my little disaster. Was it? I hope it was."

Nearby, one of the waitresses was upending the chairs, placing them on tables. "Time to go," he said.

"Where?"

"I'll show you. But we have to wait for a couple of hours until the building clears out."

"What shall we do in the meantime?" She placed her hand on top of his. "Can you think of something that might make us feel like human beings?"

He had a motel room on Route 66 a couple of miles past the campus. The sex took a long time, but she did not come. In the old days with her ex-boyfriend, she would have been okay with faking it in order to achieve her naturalized idealization—no more. No longer would she feel she had to justify a Butlerian concept of heterosexuality.

She was thinking too much about herself to find pleasure. She had helped him with the condom, making sure that he was tightly sealed. But when he pushed into her, she excited herself by imagining what it might be like to become pregnant, to experience the real deal—she loved thinking about this, in this and other contexts, but only after having first removed the possibility. This time she could not manage to sustain herself, and as the minutes passed she found his rhythmic movements had knocked something free, had liberated a series of images that had nothing to do with him or where they were, and which did nothing to comfort or pacify or fulfill her: She saw Karen Larsen, her thesis advisor at BU, in the bath of a hotel room like this one, perhaps, the same yellow walls, the water tinged with red. She had imagined this before, but now there was some other movement in the room, a quick, flitting shadow, or else a white face, briefly, in the mirror above the sink.

He took her upper lip between his lips, pulled on her nipple, but what she thought about were the figures on the steps behind her at the lecture hall. Or she imagined the innocent young face of the undergraduate seated beside her, and remembered the excitement she had once felt in the early days, puzzling over gnomic texts from the Frankfurt School—where was Adorno now? she wondered, irrelevantly. Where had he managed to hole up? And what was his lineage—Hegel via Husserl, perhaps? Could she make the dates work out? It's lucky they were such a greedy bunch, and these cushy academic appointments were so rare. Otherwise they would have infected the whole world with critical theory. But they lived forever, or almost forever, and they didn't want the competition.

After the man was finished, for a while he lay on top of her, his cheek against her shoulder. She liked that. He was not heavy. She brought up her hand to stroke his hair. Then he got up to take a shower, and she stretched her arms and legs out on the wide bed. He left the door open, and she listened to the water. She was thinking, again, in a series of images, a graphic-novel version of the past few years: herself, sitting in the kitchen of her Somerville apartment, barefoot, dressed in sweats, halfway through a bottle of Chardonnay, listening to a voicemail from her douchebag ex-boyfriend; herself, walking down Mass. Ave. toward her stupid job in the maternity store, hands in her pockets, stupid knitted cap on her head; herself, late at night, slumped forward in her study carrel in Mugar Library, her face pressed against her crossed forearms; herself in Karen Larsen's Arlington house, staring across at her kind, solicitous, angelic, baffled face, as she searched for words to describe the doomed morass that was the Kristeva dissertation, the sucking, endless, teeming, bug-infested tar pit through which both of them were doomed to wander, caught in circles, until breath gave out. No, Karen had escaped, seen her chance and taken it. Only she was left, Yvette Daume, cowering on the one dry island, no one to light the way.

She'd been wrong about Butler and apparently about Kristeva too—postanthropologic after all. She listened to the man use the toilet. He hadn't given his name and she hadn't asked for it, perhaps as a security precaution. Whistling softly, he flushed—he was proud of himself, no doubt. She, less so. The last panel, before she closed the book, was of herself, now, spread-eagled on this bed, the sheet pulled up over her big thighs. She must look terrible, she decided, her face blotched and streaked.

She took an instant to remember more precisely the young man at the lecture, the student, his black glasses, his earnest face. What if she were with him now, listening to his sounds in the bathroom? Maybe she would have been able to share something more with him. Maybe she would have been able to teach him something as he lay in her arms, his unshaved cheek against her breast. Maybe he might have had performativity issues, and she could have consoled him, though not in Butlerian terms—she was done with that. Never again. She could have explained some things, and if he'd said, "One could critique that," she could have gone—no, just think about it. Fuck critiquing it. And if he'd said, "I want to address how we frame the question," then she might have gone—no, if you want to do that, do it for a minute afterward, and not for very long. If you try it before, it ruins everything. You want to answer the question before you frame it, let alone address the frame. He would have nodded, thoughtful, and she would have felt the movement on her breast.

But what if he had said, "Is what's false an imitation of what's real? Or is it the other way?" What would she have said?

Now the actual man came in from the bathroom and smiled down at her. He often smiled, which irritated her. "Get ready," he said. "It's time to make a foray." He paused, scratched his arms, smelled his fingers, rubbed his nose. "This afternoon was just a reconnoiter." Then, after a pause: "I could be wrong about this."

"No kidding."

She hadn't seen the gun since the lecture, but now she did, a long, antique revolver as if from a John Ford western. He put on his pants and strapped the holster to the outside of his leg. He didn't turn on the lamp. Light came from the open bathroom door, and from a lantern by the office door outside, filtered through gauze curtains. "Different colleges have different what you might call nests of activity. Here it's in the Comp Lit department. That's where the measurements are outside normal levels. I've been studying the plans for Fisk Hall, where they have their offices."

"There's no Comp Lit at Wesleyan," she said.

He smiled. "Not officially. It's a secret program."

Irritated and embarrassed, she rolled out of bed, covering her breasts in her crossed arms. "Please turn around." She never liked men to watch her get dressed. He stood watching her. He had dimples. She turned away from him and sat down on the side of the bed, facing the window, to put on her brassiere. "For crying out loud."

"What?"

"A little privacy," she said, buttoning her blouse.

When she stood up, he was all business. He turned on the overhead light. Then he went out the door and she watched him open the trunk of his car. He brought in some blueprints rolled in an architect's case and spread one of them out on the surface of the bed, away from the wet spot. He dragged the bedclothes down, pushed them onto the floor. "This is the floor plan," he said. "Fisk Hall is on College and High Street. I cased it earlier. I don't have much to suggest. But Farinelli has her office here, above the Language Resource Center." He paused. "Didn't she say she was in Anthropology? That's clear on the other side of Wyllys. Two hundred and seventy-six feet away."

She was still pissed at him. "Suspicious."

He shrugged. "That's all I've got. Like I said, I don't think she is the only one. I was going to go over there and look around." He'd been bending over the bed, his finger on the plan. Now he glanced up at her. "You want to come?"

Really? she thought. For this he brought a blueprint in a fancy case? On the other hand, of course she wanted to go with him. That was why she had had sex with him: not to be left behind. Not to drive two hours back to Boston, up I-84 and to that vacant exit. At least not right away.

They put their coats on and got back into the car. On High Street it had begun to snow, a few whirling flakes. Past nine o'clock, they sat in the parked car and waited for the lights to go out on the top floor. "That's her office," he said. "Fourth from the corner."

It was nice sitting in the car with him. She reached over to squeeze his hand. "Should we go up?" he asked.

"Don't look at me. I'm banned from campus."

They talked about other stuff as well. Personal things. She teased him: "How do you know so much?"

He hesitated. "It's my girlfriend. She teaches at U. Conn. She was up for this job—Farinelli's job. They brought her for an interview, a campus talk. No chance. The wise ones have it wired up."

"So?"

"Get rid of the undead wood. Give some one else a shot."

She let go of his hand. "You have a girlfriend?"

The streets were deserted, dark. Eventually the light went out in Professor Farinelli's office, and in a few more minutes they saw her standing on the steps, peering up and down the street. Nor was it crazy or paranoid to think that she seemed nervous, ill at ease. She pulled up the faux-leopard-skin lapels of her overcoat and then crossed between the cars, catty-corner toward Wyllys Avenue and the president's house. Then she crossed to the other side where three small college buildings stood in a row, and stood for a moment outside the middle one, which was dark. She smoked part of a cigarette, flicked it away. Again glancing around her, she stepped onto the porch, unlocked the door, and slipped inside.

"Gosh," the man said. "I didn't think anyone ever went in there. That's some kind of secret society house." He jumped out of the car and ran across the street. By the time Yvette was able to follow him, he was already on the porch, pounding on the door.

"What are you doing?" she asked as she came up the walk. The building was an old one, perhaps mid-nineteenth century, with stone lintels. It was windowless, at least on this side. He was hitting the door with slow, powerful strokes, and he had his gun in his right hand. "What are you doing?" she repeated. But if he had a plan, she never found it out; the door opened. Professor Farinelli had taken off her hat and gloves. She stood partially in silhouette, the bulk of the light behind her, a soft, amber glow. But now Yvette was close enough to see a number of details she had missed that afternoon in Crowell Hall—the woman was far younger than she'd thought, perhaps a couple of years out of graduate school. And close up she was luminously beautiful, a cloud of light around her red-gold hair. And stylishly dressed, and also supernaturally quick: She'd been expecting someone, perhaps, and her tense, artificial smile had turned immediately to astonishment and then something else, a look of furious determination. Before the man could raise his hand she'd reached across the threshold, thrust her lacquered nails into his throat, pulled him forward into the chamber; he stumbled to his knees. Yvette received a quick impression of the grotesque, sucking mouth, posthuman, transhuman, antihuman, who could tell? It was the complexity of these distinctions that made modern critical theory so infuriating. She had her stiletto out now, and as Farinelli bent over the man's breast she stabbed her through the back of the neck with the silver blade. She stepped inside the room and shut the door and leaned her back against it, surveying what she'd done.

The man, of course, was dead. She hadn't even seen how that had happened. Farinelli's mouth was open and her breath was rough. Yvette had severed her spinal column as Professor Larsen had taught her, a single stroke and then a twist of the blade, as they'd practiced during breaks. It was a myth that they couldn't die, and Karen had told her to pay attention to what happened next, the transformation. She stood with her hands behind her, and again her mind had migrated to her mountain cleft, from which she could look down and examine the sprawled figure of the man, Farinelli's fingers still locked in his throat. And then there, as if far below her, lay the creature herself, flopping listlessly, a subtle haze obscuring her body, clinging like a mist to her yellow cashmere sweater, her bare shoulders. She must have stripped off her overcoat as soon as she had stepped inside.

The door behind Yvette was heavy and dark. She raised her arms now and grabbed hold of something above her, a sigil carved into the surface. Below her, Farinelli writhed and twitched as her flesh receded, as her arms and legs dried into brittle sticks. Yvette could see the sinews coursing down her neck as the submerged fat melted from her acromion and scapula. Her tongue withered in her mouth, and Yvette could hear, disappearing as if on the wind, her final words a garbled remnant of something she had said that afternoon: "Through a discussion of bodily suffering, I see eroticism as integral to a deconstruction . . . a dissolution of the subject . . ."

And that was that. The creature, ancient, a dry, disassembled, deconstructed husk, was dead. Yvette had been jabbing the point of the stiletto into the wood behind her, while with her left hand she had grabbed hold of the skull-and-serpent sigil above her head. Now she let go and stepped away from the entwined figures farther into the room. Stiletto clutched, she made a circuit of the chamber, examining the mix of gothic and modern furnishing: glass-fronted cabinets, partial skeletons, stuffed animals, ripped armchairs and sofas around a flat-screen TV, a litter of Xboxes and PS3s—gamer's grotto meets high-Victorian camp. She saw a number of books, poststructuralist classics, backs broken, face down, strewn about on the scarred coffee table amid the dirty cups: *The Gift of Death*, *Empire of Signs*, *Hatred and Forgiveness*, *A Taste for the Secret*, *The Pleasures of Repetition*. Paul de Man's *The Resistance to Theory* was among them, the pages decorated with coffee rings. Light came from a low brass lampstand with a beaded shade, which left the far recesses of the chamber in obscurity. But now Yvette could see something moving back there, something spread out on the surface of a table or makeshift altar: marble top, mahogany veneer.

She took her time. She imagined leaving this place, shutting the door, walking down the hill again to find her car parked on Main Street in front of the bank. She had to work in the morning at the maternity store in Somerville. That wasn't the worst thing, was it, under the circumstances? She examined her feelings, while at the same time she took little steps that brought her closer to the table under the blocked-up window, where among the tarnished candelabra she could see the desiccated figure of a man, curled up on himself and the narrow surface, chained down, she saw, with iron cuffs—that was the sound she'd heard.

His head was hairless, an animated skull. She leaned down to hear him speak, the soft words unintelligible, because her German never had been good. But he must have smelled her; now he opened his eyes, and now the words came clear, his accent thick at first, then dwindling. "She's starving me. I was the one who hired her, over some objections I may say. The decision was not unanimous. And now what has she done? Please," he whispered, and she could see his delicate nostrils flare. "I am so hungry. So . . . thirsty."

Yvette brought up the stiletto and laid it across his bare esophagus, just has Karen had shown her. But then she hesitated. And perhaps he could sense the hesitation: "You," he said. "Please, please. I have under my control a two-year postdoc, what do you say? Or if your dissertation is not finished, perhaps we could arrange something . . . under my supervision. The stipend is . . . quite generous . . ."

"What's the teaching load?" she whispered, her breath as soft as his.

"Teaching . . ." he said, almost too weak to continue, until she brought her wrist up to his lips, and allowed his little, childlike mouth to fasten onto it. After a moment she could feel his rough, probing tongue.

A Homily for Good Friday

Brothers and sisters, join in imitating me, and
observe those who live according to the example of
have in us. For many live as enemies of the cross of
Christ; I have often told you of them, and now I tell
you even with tears. Their end is their destruction,
their god is the belly, and their glory is in their
shame; their minds are set on earthly things.
—St. Paul's Letter to the Philippians, 3:17

WE CAN READ THIS excerpt from the letter to the Philippians as part of a fight over the future of the early church. On one side, St. Paul's mission to the gentiles. On the other, James and Peter and their followers, who don't think it necessary to give up their Jewish traditions in order to embrace Jesus. These are the people Paul calls enemies of the cross of Christ. As he says, "Their god is the belly, and their glory is in their shame." That is, they follow the dietary laws of Moses and the custom of circumcision. For Paul, this means they are obsessed with earthly things and with their own attempts to purify themselves, instead of trusting the redemption Jesus offers them.

For Paul, Christianity is a simple thing, easily summarized. "All I want is to know Christ and the power of his resurrection, and to share his sufferings by becoming like him in his death." We too, primed by anti-Semitism, can easily find ways to congratulate ourselves, that we have not let ourselves be distracted by the letter of the law to the detriment of faith, which should be the law's foundation. We, like Paul, indeed like Jesus, can sneer at those ancient Pharisees. But I ask you to imagine ways that we're the same as they are. Since theology abhors a vacuum, a great deal has grown up inside the church in the past two millennia to replace what Paul tried so majestically to clear away. Whenever I stand to recite the Nicene Creed, for example, I think to myself, this is our proliferated law, not of ritual purity, but of belief.

In a way it's natural to confuse belief with faith. Faith cannot be discussed, cannot be described. But we've got to discuss something with all the time we have to kill, so we fall back on belief. We believe this. We believe that. If you don't believe this, you're not one of us. But belief is faith's opposite, if you can imagine calling one twin the opposite of the other. The similarities make the differences more crucial.

Belief comes from our heads, faith from our hearts. Belief is of this earth, faith is not. I imagine Paul to have been a world-champion doubter, and I think he would have been astonished to hear about the things Christians have been asked to believe in the centuries after his death. Things that never would have occurred to him. But the proliferation of belief is a natural process, sort of like raising the bar during an athletic competition. "You think that's hard—try this. Not only was she a virgin, but she rose up to heaven in her own body."

Finally, of course, the bar is so high that we all fail in our heart of hearts. And this makes me think that the church fathers who guided this process, as well as those old Pharisees, might have been on to something. As St. Paul puts it, "This one thing I do: forgetting what lies behind and straining forward to what lies ahead. I press on toward the goal." He doesn't need to be reminded that the race cannot be won even by saints.

I'm in danger of mixing athletic metaphors here, but perhaps it's just as well for us not to think we're in the same competition as St. Paul. For the rest of us, it's good to place that bar firmly out of reach, so that we knock it down each time. Each time we pray, each time we say the Creed. In the same way, I imagine, those who follow the Jewish dietary laws and yet are mercilessly honest with themselves, must think with every bite that they are committing some impurity. Their bar is also too high.

We need to be reminded every day, but especially on Good Friday, of the spiritual importance of failure. On Easter we have a different celebration, but today is our day of failure. And not to put too fine a point on it, but it's Christ's day of failure too. It's the day when it became clear to him that no one, not Peter, not John, not Mary his mother or Mary Magdalene, and certainly not any of us, were able to believe what he was telling them, even after years of trying. In a way, he was the most incompetent messiah in the history of the world. As we have seen so painfully in these past years, over and over, the most unlikely prophets can find people who follow them to death. It was no different then. Josephus describes several messianic movements from the generation after Christ, all of which resulted in massacres. Christ's movement is unique in that no one believed in it at all, at least not enough to die with him. And maybe that's a feature of the truth, that it cannot be believed with any certainty. If something inspires certainty, then it has to be a lie.

Or maybe it's just that doubt comes from doubt and certainty from certainty, and only false prophets are sure. The words from the cross show a range of feeling, from certainty to despair. A range of concerns, some earthly, some sublime. If we are, in Paul's phrase, "to share Christ's suffering by being like him in his death," then maybe we should share his doubts as well. Maybe that's the worst of what he suffered.

Or there is a third possibility. Why would Jesus have wanted Peter to accept him, if it meant he might be tortured and killed? Surely that would also be a sign of a false prophet. Maybe when Jesus says to Peter, "You will deny me," he should take it not as a prophecy, but as a command. Maybe he was saying even then, that it is through failure of belief that we find faith.

Creative Nonfiction

HE NEVER WOULD HAVE guessed she was the type to play these games. One of his prompts was always to make him smile, maybe from some piece of misdirection or irony, and in that patch of sky she did not shine. Occasionally he'd seen her laughing with her friends or teammates outside the library. Once after dark he'd caught her as he passed through the quadrangle. She stood by herself under the chandelier in one of the side rooms of Burrell Hall. He watched her through the lighted window and she was open toward him under glass. He knew she couldn't see him because of how windows work. He stepped back out of the rhombus of light. Her blond hair, pulled back so sharply from her forehead that you could see the strain, was in a ponytail. Under the hard light her face looked pink and scrubbed. She was wearing a fleece pullover and black running tights. She turned and put her hands on her hips. Her name was Taylor McLeef, which made her sound like someone in a story. She was eighteen years old. It was a damp September evening and he was walking to his car.

Where she excelled was straight-up earnestness. Her father had died when she was young. Her mother was a lawyer. She played on the field hockey team. He knew these and many other details of her life because of the nature of the class she took on Tuesday and Thursday afternoons, Creative Nonfiction.

She had not yet figured out the "creative" part, and she was not alone. He'd seen hundreds like her, students who succeeded by following directions, a forced march that started in elementary school. There was something inhuman about them, or transhuman at least, a master race of female student athletes, filing past him like robots into the future. Taylor's work was single-minded, uninflected, autobiographical. Here is an example:

> I came out the restroom hating myself all over, the taste of barf and acid in my throat, and found a room where I could be alone. Because of the light from the fixture, I could see my reflection thrown back, my mouth open because of the pain in my throat. I hated what I looked like. But then I could see (and it didn't make me feel better!) Mr. Santelli peering in at me from the walkway in the quad. What a little creep! I turned to show him my fat ass, and when I turned back he was gone. I hate him and I hate his stupid class. He's way big on telling the truth, way big on self-exposure. Now I can see why!

As a distancing mechanism, he had suggested writing about herself from a different point of view, or else in the third person. Then she could describe things she hadn't actually seen or heard. "It's not meant to be a record of what really happened," he'd told her more than once.

A man of medium height, popular with students and faculty, Mike had been working at the school for six years since his divorce. He lived in a one-bedroom apartment in the town, five miles or so from campus. It was there at the kitchen table that he corrected student papers over a bottle of merlot. Was this a step forward or a step backward? Could it be called "creative" to misinterpret everything, or call yourself fat when you were thin, popular when you were not?

But Jesus, what was this?

I know how to get back at him. I have a mandatory conference next week in his office. He's been giving me crappy grades and I've put Mom on the case. But I can do more. If he wants to look, let him look. He likes my black leggings, I'll wear my black leggings. And maybe something sexy on the top.

It was true. He did have a meeting with Taylor the next Monday morning in his office above the library. And on Friday he had gotten an email from his department chair, telling him that Winifred McLeef, who was an alumna of the school and a former trustee, had some concerns about her daughter. Could he provide some clarification on her progress in his class?

He sat up late on Sunday night. The next morning, when Taylor came in at ten o'clock, he scarcely looked at her. Yes, he verified what she was wearing. She sat down in the chair next to his desk and he went over his comments: "These seem like random events, random thoughts and feelings. It's not a travelogue, this happened and then this happened and then that happened. You need a plot. That's the difference between stories and real life."

He risked a glimpse at her face. She looked like a caricature of puzzlement, furrowed brow, pursed lips. To all appearances she was a serious girl, serious about her future, or at least her GPA. "It's not finished," she said. "She hasn't even decided what to do."

"To punish him, you mean."

"Yes. I mean she's teasing him a little bit."

"I don't like that part," he said. "Which means I don't believe it. It's not in character."

He kept his eyes on her paper, the marked-up pages spread out on the desk. "It's not like she's some kind of teenaged seductress. You haven't built that into her. She's too insecure."

"I didn't mean . . ." She paused and then she stopped.

"Then what about this?" he asked, indicating the phrase "maybe something sexy" with his red pencil. "Every detail is important. I don't even know why she's got it in for this poor guy. What's his name? Santelli?"

"He spied on her. He gave her a bad grade."

"Honestly, I don't think that's enough motivation. He could have just been walking to his car. He could have glanced in through the window, not even seen her. Sometimes when you're inside a room at dusk, say, you think people can see you when they can't. You don't know how the light affects the glass."

"He gave her a B."

"But she deserved it! She knows that! The way you've written her, she's young, but she's not unfair. She's not about to ruin someone's life just because she doesn't like him."

People had tried to ruin his life before, his ex-wife in particular. He felt Taylor's gaze on the side of his face. She was only a few feet away; the office was tiny, a square of white cinderblock. Just to cross his legs was a potential harassment suit. "It all starts with character," he said. "Motivation. What does she want? Why does she want it? What happens if she doesn't get it? What happens when she does?"

This was a prepackaged spiel. "That's why I'm giving you a B on this," he said. "It's just not credible so far. High-achieving mother. A lot of pressure. Absent father. Fine. But this part, this totally mistaken body image. It doesn't add up. How does that work with the whole exhibitionism thing?"

"I don't think that's contradictory."

He risked a longer glance at her. She hadn't changed her hair at all. She still had that peeled look, her tight ponytail. Her top had a lace neck, and he could see the dark straps of her bra. But she hadn't gone for naked shoulders or even naked arms. The whole ensemble was more cautious, maybe, than she knew.

Cruelly, he pressed on. "This suggestion of bulimia. It's a cliché. I guess I don't believe that either. Not how it's written, at least."

She pressed her lips together, hollowed her cheeks. And you had to give her credit. She did seem to be thinking this through. "Yes, okay. What about this for a plot? I could make her ruthless. You know, really do it. Accuse him of all kinds of things. Lean on her mother to get him fired just for the fun of it. It's not like he has tenure."

"I guess it depends on the effect you want," he said after an extended pause. "But wouldn't we have to think she was a jerk? I don't know if the piece works if all our sympathy is with him. You know, as a whole.

"I mean," he said, "we don't want to think she's spoiled and entitled and self-absorbed, and has it in for this guy for no reason. There are worse things in the world than bad grades. I guess he could give her a D. That might help. Do you want to try that?"

"No. Absolutely not."

And then in a moment, mimicking him, "It's not credible. She's applying to colleges."

The top she wore was gray with a flowered motif. She touched her fingers to her cheek. "She seems spoiled to you?"

He shrugged. "I'm just saying we can't hate her. And you're starting at a disadvantage. Most readers have a bias against these girls at expensive private schools. To be frank, it's hard to care about their problems. This part where she hates the place so much she wants to blow it up. That seems really extreme."

Mixtures of emotion passed over her face, even though it didn't move. He said, "What you have to remember about writing, it's not about self-expression, not really. That's why Santelli's wrong. It's not about exposure. It's not about the truth. Nobody really cares what you think or feel."

She closed her mouth. He listened to the air whistle through her nose. She was puzzling it out. You had to give her credit. "Okay, so that plot won't work," she said. "It's true, I want people to like her. But what about if he's the jerk? You know, a bad man. The antagonist. Then he'd deserve whatever happened!"

He considered this. "Then he'd deserve to, say, get fired?"

"If he was bad enough. Or even worse! End up in jail. I agree with you about the harassment stuff. He's just a little creep. This isn't what this is about."

Panic moved through him. But he couldn't exactly disagree. She was right, and he couldn't pretend she wasn't. "I certainly think it's a good idea if you undercut him in some way. That way our sympathy is not about her vulnerabilities. It's about her strength."

She pulled at the flimsy fabric around her collarbone and then got up from her chair. "He could be involved in something shady. Or some kind of trauma that makes him act irrationally. A violent past. Thanks, Mr. Pombo! You've given me a lot to think about. This isn't finished, of course. I'll have a rewrite by Thursday."

Even on Wednesday, though, she seemed different to him as he saw her around school. Maybe she had gained a little weight, was that possible? At an exposition of extracurriculars outside the cafeteria (where he saw her answering questions under a banner that read *Transhumanity: The Next Evolutionary Step?*) he learned she was a Big Sister to a couple of disabled kids, and on Tuesday evenings she read local newspapers to the blind. On Wednesday morning she was with some of her teammates outside the library, protesting the new regulations on African refugees and the president's new task force on deportations, authorization for which was winding through the House of Representatives.

But that day he wasn't paying her as much attention, which was just as well. He had his own problems. Because of the conditions of his divorce he was not able to see his children, Sadiya and Mike Jr., except under supervision. But at the same time his monthly child support necessitated making more money. So he had taken on some independent tutoring and even some government work at the internment facility farther out on Long Island. He had met his wife in Cameroon and now, because of his military and state department background, he had gotten hired as an independent contractor to help process refugees, which was discouraging but necessary. The United States could not continue to be the dumping ground for half the world because of drought in the Sahel.

The camp was on the site of an old sports stadium in Stony Brook, ringed now with barbed wire. But the banks of xenon lights atop thirty-foot posts illuminated the whole space in a bluish glare. Even from the gate where he presented his identification booklet, he could hear the PA system making periodic sputtering announcements. "Please be careful of the artificial surface," he heard now. "Do not sit on the equipment monitors."

Inside, however, all was chaos—men, women, and children in the stands and on the field or in any vacant space between the structures and fence, on blankets or on pieces of cardboard, surrounded by suitcases or plastic bags full of possessions. There were lines for the port-a-potties and a stinking miasma over the entire camp. Mike parked in the lot and pushed through the crowds waiting outside the old coaches' offices, one of which he'd been assigned for the evening shift, a small, white-cinderblock room with a desk and a swivel-back chair. He was checking on immigration status under several exemptions and getting more and more frustrated until the last woman came in and shut the door, a Nigerian this time, so English-speaking, a Muslim, he guessed, with her hair wrapped up in blue cloth—he didn't even know what she was doing here. She wasn't on his list. She ignored the chair where she was supposed to sit and instead she got up in his grill: "You know I have a lawyer here, pro bono. She's been giving me advice. And she tells me you're a bad man, a very bad man. You don't care about us. Instead you have disgusting thoughts about a woman young enough to be your daughter. You harass her and then you punish her with evil grades. Why do you have to be like that? I tell you we will not forgive this situation, none of us."

He'd gotten to his feet and she'd pressed him back against the wall. It was too much. It was too fucking much. Jesus, she had her finger in his face. At that moment she looked like his ex-wife to him.

That was Wednesday night. On Thursday afternoon Taylor waited for him before class. "I know I promised, but I'm having some trouble with the rewrite," she confessed. "Is it okay if I really exaggerate things?"

"Well," he said, not wanting to set her off. "Maybe a little. But you might want to keep the story in the realm of possibility."

"But who knows where that is anymore? Did I tell you my mom is an attorney? So I put her on the case! You know, for verisimilitude. I'm inventing a whole backstory. I'm thinking the guy must have left a paper trail. And it turns out he did! His ex-wife filed a battery complaint. There was a restraining order. So now he has to work two jobs. And you know what?"

"What?" he murmured.

"I'm thinking he might work as a debriefer in one of the displaced persons' camps on the North Shore."

He held up his hands. "Okay, just remember. Keep it in the realm."

"Ooh, Mr. Pombo. What did you do to your knuckles? Did you cut yourself?"

During class, striding back and forth at the end of the room, he tried to make the point that the creative aspect of the work had to serve the purpose of the nonfiction—that is, it did not consist of invention for its own sake but as a way to strengthen and clarify reality, which was the point of the entire exercise. But Taylor had her hand up. As he ignored her and took another question from someone else, she pulled her ponytail back and fixed it in a scrunchie. She held her pencil between her teeth, and when her hair was fixed she held it up again. Even from the front of the room he could see how she had scarred and nibbled it so that the middle wasn't even yellow anymore.

"Mr. Pombo, does it have to be like that? Does it have to be that you are trying to, like, strengthen and clarify reality? Couldn't you, like, be trying to create a mood? Or maybe make a social argument? Or even just go on a journey somewhere, a crazy adventure?"

After class he walked to his office above the library and shut the door. The phone rang. "Mike," said a throaty voice he recognized. "Bad news. Apparently she's pressing charges for intimidation. And not just her. Because there is some bitch of an attorney with a hard-on about this. I'm sorry. I'm telling you as a friend."

Considering his options, Mike Pombo sat back in his padded swivel chair. Time passed, marked by the recorded announcement that the library was closed. Hours later when it was dark he heard a sliding sound, some papers pushed under his door. He leapt up, took two steps, yanked at the knob. But there was no one in the dark hallway.

He saw on the first page of the essay at his feet, in a careful line down the left-hand side, a trio of blue post-its. #1: "I just wanted to try something new. Let me know if it works!" #2: "PS, I really appreciate you taking the time. I told my mother about it." #3: "You were right. It's not about the girl's problems, it's about his. I feel so much better!"

Her handwriting, which he had not seen before, was minuscule and exact. He allowed himself a groan. Yes, her mother could get him fired, but he'd be damned before he read any more of this tonight. And he had no desire to see how she had decided to humiliate Mr. Santelli, for whom he was beginning to feel not just sympathy but empathy, a distinction he felt sure Taylor was incapable of grasping. No, that was unfair. It was just the sort of thing she'd memorized for the SAT.

But he leafed through the pages to see if she had made the page requirement. She hadn't, and the text sprawled away into a curt, hopeful, parenthetical "to be continued."

Undecided, he hefted his briefcase in his right hand. Then he laid the essay on the metal surface of the desk and laid the briefcase over it, snapping it shut over the arming mechanism. Then he hurried out into the deserted parking lot. It was ten thirty at night. The school was at the top of a hill, and he took the long drive through the dark trees to Rte. 25A. There he turned left in his gray Subaru. In the dark interior, lit by red circle on the dashboard, he found himself contained in a bleak, grim, brooding mood, the kind that came up out of nowhere sometimes when he measured what he used to have against what he had now. At such moments—here along the straightaway—he often felt himself drift up out of the world and into a soft airless space, a non-alcoholic drunkenness that deadened his response to his own body or the evidence of his own senses. When he heard the police siren behind him and saw the flashing lights he thought immediately that he must have been speeding, and then immediately afterward that he'd be pulled over and arrested because of the Nigerian woman from Kano who had baited him the night before. But how could that be? He'd barely touched her. He skidded to a stop on the gravel shoulder but then the patrol car sped past him, and then another, and then another one while he sat back and tried to breathe. With his eyes closed he could still see for a moment, until it vanished up ahead, the rhythmic flash.

During the riots in Cameroon he had seen a building blow out into the street. Head ringing, dizzy, he had dug through the concrete and shattered glass, looking for corpses and survivors. Now he wondered whether if some kind of deranged person attacked the school, he would feel a concussive blast even at this distance. With his eyes closed he imagined Taylor's uncompleted essay atomize into burning mist, the window of his office bursting out, and maybe, if he was lucky, the roof collapsing on that entire section of the building. He imagined a plume of fire above the trees.

Hands shaking, he started the car and pulled it out onto the road. He had part of an idea that if the police were to come for him because of some violation, he would pack some clothes from his apartment and drive away somewhere, maybe down to Florida, maybe to Key West or Daytona Beach, an idiotic plan, the kind of plan that might appeal not to an ex-SOF with two tours in Syria, but to an ignorant seventeen-year-old, say, specifically a seventeen-year-old girl who didn't know fuck-all and didn't have children of her own.

Two miles ahead as he came into town, he saw the police barricade across the road and a dozen figures in hazmat suits, their faces hidden behind plastic shields. Blue light spread from some indefinite source. He stopped the car, rolled down the window. Behind him he could hear the whine of fire engines. One of the women pulled her mask to one side. She poked her long flashlight through the window and informed Mike that this whole area and much of the North Shore was under quarantine.

"Can I go home?" With his chin, he motioned up ahead past the barricade.

"License and registration."

While he waited, Mike thought about what might come up on the computer. He checked his phone. But the main story from the *New York Times* website was that the North Korean government had issued some kind of ultimatum in response to the blockade. This was in the context of a general diplomatic breakdown on the peninsula.

The woman came back. "You're on our list," she said. "We're sending you to a clinic in Port Washington to get checked out. There's been an outbreak of a necrotizing virus from West Africa." She mentioned the detention center where Mike worked.

"Can I drive myself?"

"I guess. It doesn't really matter anymore."

Which is not what you want to hear from someone in hazmat gear. Maybe Daytona Beach wasn't such a bad idea.

The woman gave him the address to the clinic and he turned the car around. But where he should have gone left he went right, away from the coast toward the expressway. He glanced at his scraped knuckles. Something else to worry about. Not to mention the chance of nuclear war. His brother Raymond lived in Seattle, within range. He thought about putting in a call.

Darkness on the little road in the scrub forest. Up ahead, a single streetlight and a telephone pole. And a girl there waiting. She knew he'd come. She wasn't hitchhiking. But she stood out on the road with her hands up and he stopped the car.

She looked different. She didn't have any of that tight preppy look, not anymore. She was dressed in green cargo pants, for God's sake, Doc Martens, and a hooded sweatshirt. Her hair was loose and wild. She was wearing eye make-up streaked with tears.

She got in, and he drove south down the deserted road. He grunted. "How does it end?"

"You didn't read it?"

"I skimmed. It looked unfinished."

"I know. It's really hard." She started to cry, an irritating sound because it seemed so unlike her, as weird as the pants and the makeup and the unbrushed hair. But what had he said to them just a few days ago? "Maybe show conflicting attributes in every scene."

She peered ahead into the moving cones of light. Her face was lumpy and slack. "You gave us options. I thought I'd just go crazy and extreme."

He'd been driving fast, but now he let the Subaru slow down as he crested the long straight hill. "But I'm sorry I didn't make the page requirement," she confessed, her head against the glass of the side window. "I hope it won't affect my grade. I didn't know how to end it. I mean I thought about him ending up in jail. Looking back, I guess, regretful. But still unable to claim responsibility. Always blaming other people."

"What had he done? Maybe let's start there."

"Maybe it doesn't matter. I'll get my mother to defend him. Pro bono."

"Really? What if it's for transporting a minor across state lines? You know, to Florida."

"I'm almost eighteen." She had started to cry again—no sobs. Just tears on her face. "But I have to tell you. The craziest thing wasn't even the new virus. It was more local."

Ahead of them the road curved to the right. He slowed to about ten miles an hour to make the turn. He'd seen movement through the trees. And when the road straightened out again he tapped the brake, rolled to a stop.

"What about the bomb in the briefcase?" he asked.

"My mom says not to judge him. He's probably seen terrible things. She says PTSD is like a new kind of evolution. There doesn't even have to be a war."

He nodded. "Oh, she does?" And then in a moment, "You know it's the girl who has a problem with the school. He's grateful just to have a job."

He peered out through the windshield. They were only a few miles from the crossroad to his ex's house. But the way was blocked. "He was just embassy security in Yaoundé," he lied. "Why would he know anything about explosives? There's more tension if the bomb never goes off."

He watched her consider this. Maybe there were ways to manage the situation. He was the grownup, after all, the teacher. But what the fuck. "What am I looking at here?"

She seemed calmer now, less weepy all of a sudden, almost proud of herself. "Trans-humans," she said. "Runaways. The rest have come up from the swamps."

He turned around to back up. But others had come out of the trees, cast in red from the brake lights. One was very tall, very thin, and as Mike watched through the rear window, she put her hand on the car, a clicking sound.

In the front seat, Taylor McLeef turned toward him. "Mr. Pombo," she said, "don't turn us loose. Unlock the doors."

"Please," she added, after a moment.

And as he complied, she murmured all in a rush, "It's been so hard for me at school. Don't judge me—I can't even eat the food. The food in the dining commons, it literally makes me sick. Not enough engine oil or something. I have to cough it out—it doesn't have the nutrients I need. But I can't talk to my adviser about that. You're the only one who understands."

Another girl climbed in the back, a second member of the field hockey team. He studied her face in the rear-view. Sometimes he had watched the home games from the sidelines, even the practices when he could get away with it. He liked the athleticism, the ponytails swishing back and forth.

Outside the car, spectral figures shambled out of the glare of the headlights or moved into the woods. One of them collapsed down the embankment into a ditch, and even from inside the car Mike could hear the clatter. "So," he said, making conversation. "Taylor can predict the future. What about you?"

He didn't expect an answer. But the girl in the back seat (pale, red-haired, faintly Goth) wrinkled her nose. "Reverse-stick drive from the top of the circle. I can hook the ball for thirty yards."

"And yet you lost to . . ." He mentioned the school's archrivals.

The girl shrugged. "Are you kidding me? Those freaks are more ceramic than meat. You should see them in the locker room. We have to flush the perchlorate out of the hypos when they're done."

In the rear-view, Mike examined the glint of metal under her ear, the hinged, chiseled jaw. He couldn't tell if it was makeup or else makeup scraped away. In the front seat, Taylor shook her head. "This is exactly the kind of bigotry we try to—"

Mike interrupted her. "What else?"

"I eat broken glass without hurting my mouth," said the girl in the back seat. "It's a family thing. My mother had it."

An air force jet ripped low over the trees above the car, headed toward New York. Mike waited for a moment till the noise had cleared. "That's all?"

She wouldn't meet his eyes in the rear-view. Her voice was soft and whispery. "Hide things. Make people miss."

He put his hands back on the steering wheel, flexed his fingers, which were sore, the knuckles a purple color, the torn skin angry and inflamed. "Okay," he said. "What now?"

"Down here at the crossroads a few miles," said Taylor. "Take a left. There's a ranch-style house at the bottom of a cul-de-sac. You'll see." She rubbed her nose, examined her fingers. "I feel like Siri."

"Okay. Sure."

"Power's out," breathed the girl in the back seat.

He put the car in gear. This stretch of road, he'd driven down it many times, back and forth without making the turn. Another plane passed overhead. He was creeping along, five or ten miles an hour. Small woods separated the houses. No light anywhere. At the crossroad, the streetlight flickered and went out.

And when they got to Simone's house a mile beyond the turn, her windows were dark too. But her car was there, a Subaru that matched his own. He pulled off next to it. Above them, when he turned off the engine and killed the lights, the night sky was full of stars, which in this part of Suffolk County was a sign of the apocalypse.

Bibliography

Publications (novels and chapter book novellas, first English-language editions):
Soldiers of Paradise (novel, Arbor House, 1987)
Sugar Rain (novel, William Morrow, 1989)
The Cult of Loving Kindness (novel, William Morrow, 1991)
Coelestis (novel, Harper Collins UK, 1994)
The Gospel of Corax (novel, Soho Books, 1996)
Three Marys (novel, Cosmos Books, 2000)
No Traveller Returns (novella, PS Publishing, 2004)
A Princess of Roumania (novel, Tor Books, 2005)
The Tourmaline (novel, Tor Books, 2006)
The White Tyger (novel, Tor Books, 2007)
The Hidden World (novel, Tor Books, 2008)
The Rose of Sarifal (published under the pseudonym Paulina Claiborne, Wizards of the Coast, 2012)
Ghosts Doing the Orange Dance (novella, PS Publishing, 2013)
All Those Vanished Engines (novel, Tor Books, 2014)

Story collections:
If Lions Could Speak (Wildside Press, 2002)
Other Stories (PS Publishing, 2015)
A City Made of Words (PM Press, 2019)

Short fiction:
"Rangriver Fell" (1987)
"Carbontown" (1989)
"The Village in the Trees" (1991)
"The Lost Sepulcher of Huáscar Capac" (1992)
"A Man on Crutches" (1994)
"The Tourist" (1994)
"The Breakthrough" (1995)
"The Last Homosexual" (1996)
"Get a Grip" (1997)
"Bukavu Dreams" (1999)
"Untitled 4" (2000)
"Self Portrait, with Melanoma, Final Draft" (2001)
"Tachycardia" (2002)
"If Lions Could Speak" (2002)
"Christmas in Jaisalmer" (2002)
"Abduction" (2002)
"No Traveller Returns" (2004)
"Fragrant Goddess" (2007)
"The Blood of Peter Francisco" (2008)
"A Family History" (2009)
"Watchers at the Living Gate" (2010)
"The Persistence of Memory, or This Space for Sale" (2010)
"Ghosts Doing the Orange Dance" (2010)
"Mysteries of the Old Quarter" (2011)

"The Microscopic Eye" (2012)
"Cho Oyu Glacier" (2012)
"The Statue in the Garden" (2013)
"The Mermaid and the Fisherman" (2014)
"A Resistance to Theory" (2014)
"Blind Spot" (2016)
"Creative Nonfiction" (2018)
"Excerpts: Naming Mt. Thoreau" (2018)
"Climate Change" (2019)
"A Conversation with the Author" (2019)
"Dear Sir or Madam" (2019)

These stories have appeared in various magazines and anthologies: *Fence*, *Omni*, *Asimov's Science Fiction*, *The Magazine of Fantasy and Science Fiction*, *Postscripts*, *Conjunctions*, *Interzone*, *Lightspeed*, and *Strange Plasma*. They have been published or else reprinted in thirty or so anthologies, either themed or best-of-the-year. My nonfiction has appeared in the *L.A. Times*, the *Richmond Times-Dispatch*, and the *New York Review of Science Fiction*, among other publications.

Translations:
Various of my novels and short stories have appeared in Spanish, German, Polish, French, Czech, and Japanese, as well as in numerous UK editions.

Poetry:
A long narrative poem, *Ragnarok*, a pseudo-Norse pseudo-edda, was published on Tor.com in April 2011 and then reprinted in three later anthologies.

Museum shows:

I provided the text for a permanent sound installation on the site of the old power plant at MASS MoCA, a collaboration with the artist Stephen Vitiello. It opened in the fall of 2011.

In the fall of 2017, I completed a second piece with Mr. Vitiello, a sound installation at a new city museum in West Palm Beach, Florida, on the site of an empty department store.

Awards:

My novels, short stories, and poems have been shortlisted for the following prizes: the Nebula Award (twice), the World Fantasy Award (three times), the Arthur C. Clarke Award, the British Science Fiction Award, the James R. Tiptree Award (twice), the Sidewise Award for Alternate History (twice), the Locus Readers' Award (twice), the Rhysling Poetry Award, the International Horror Guild Award, the Shirley Jackson Award, and the Theodore Sturgeon Award (twice). *The Cult of Loving Kindness* was a *New York Times* Notable Book.

About the Author

A NATIVE OF NEW England with Southern roots, Paul Park climaxed his "wanderjahr" in Asia and the Middle East with his *Sugar Rain Trilogy*, which established him immediately as a writer to watch. His fascinated readers have since followed him into Christian theology, the anatomy of colonialism, and the limits and possibilities of metafictional narrative. His diverse work includes narrations of museum exhibits with sound artist Stephen Vitiello, and lectures on storytelling at New York Comic Con and nonhuman sentience at Berlin's Max Planck Institute. Meanwhile he has taught writing at several universities. He lives in western Massachusetts and currently teaches at Williams College, where he is both worshipped and feared.

FRIENDS OF

PM

These are indisputably momentous times—the financial system is melting down globally and the Empire is stumbling. Now more than ever there is a vital need for radical ideas.

In the years since its founding—and on a mere shoestring—PM Press has risen to the formidable challenge of publishing and distributing knowledge and entertainment for the struggles ahead. With hundreds of releases to date, we have published an impressive and stimulating array of literature, art, music, politics, and culture. Using every available medium, we've succeeded in connecting those hungry for ideas and information to those putting them into practice.

Friends of PM allows you to directly help impact, amplify, and revitalize the discourse and actions of radical writers, filmmakers, and artists. It provides us with a stable foundation from which we can build upon our early successes and provides a much-needed subsidy for the materials that can't necessarily pay their own way. You can help make that happen—and receive every new title automatically delivered to your door once a month—by joining as a Friend of PM Press. And, we'll throw in a free T-shirt when you sign up.

Here are your options:

- $30 a month: Get all books and pamphlets plus 50% discount on all webstore purchases
- $40 a month: Get all PM Press releases (including CDs and DVDs) plus 50% discount on all webstore purchases
- $100 a month: Superstar—Everything plus PM merchandise, free downloads, and 50% discount on all webstore purchases

For those who can't afford $30 or more a month, we have Sustainer Rates at $15, $10, and $5. Sustainers get a free PM Press T-shirt and a 50% discount on all purchases from our website.

Your Visa or Mastercard will be billed once a month, until you tell us to stop. Or until our efforts succeed in bringing the revolution around. Or the financial meltdown of Capital makes plastic redundant. Whichever comes first.

PM Press was founded at the end of 2007 by a small collection of folks with decades of publishing, media, and organizing experience. PM Press co-conspirators have published and distributed hundreds of books, pamphlets, CDs, and DVDs. Members of PM have founded enduring book fairs, spearheaded victorious tenant organizing campaigns, and worked closely with bookstores, academic conferences, and even rock bands to deliver political and challenging ideas to all walks of life. We're old enough to know what we're doing and young enough to know what's at stake.

We seek to create radical and stimulating fiction and nonfiction books, pamphlets, T-shirts, visual and audio materials to entertain, educate, and inspire you. We aim to distribute these through every available channel with every available technology—whether that means you are seeing anarchist classics at our bookfair stalls; reading our latest vegan cookbook at the café; downloading geeky fiction e-books; or digging new music and timely videos from our website.

PM Press is always on the lookout for talented and skilled volunteers, artists, activists, and writers to work with. If you have a great idea for a project or can contribute in some way, please get in touch.

PM Press
PO Box 23912
Oakland, CA 94623
510-658-3906 • info@pmpress.org

PM Press in Europe
europe@pmpress.org
www.pmpress.org.uk

Report from Planet Midnight

Nalo Hopkinson
$12.00
ISBN: 978-1-60486-497-7
5 by 7.5 • 128 pages

Nalo Hopkinson has been busily (and wonderfully) "subverting the genre" since her first novel, *Brown Girl in the Ring*, won a Locus Award for SF and Fantasy in 1999. Since then she has acquired a prestigious World Fantasy Award, a legion of adventurous and aware fans, a reputation for intellect seasoned with humor, and a place of honor in the short list of SF writers who are tearing down the walls of category and transporting readers to previously unimagined planets and realms.

Never one to hold her tongue, Hopkinson takes on sexism and racism in publishing in "Report from Planet Midnight," a historic and controversial presentation to her colleagues and fans.

Plus... "Message in a Bottle," a radical new twist on the time travel tale that demolishes the sentimental myth of childhood innocence; and "Shift," a tempestuous erotic adventure in which Caliban gets the girl. Or does he?

And Featuring: our Outspoken Interview, an intimate one-on-one that delivers a wealth of insight, outrage, irreverence, and top-secret Caribbean spells.

Fire.

Elizabeth Hand
$13.00
ISBN: 978-1-62963-234-6
5 by 7.5 • 128 pages

Hand, Elizabeth, or Liz as she's known to her colleagues, students, and devoted fans, is a maverick in modern fiction: a fearless literary sojourner whose award-winning novels and short stories mix murder and magic, high fantasy and post-punk noir in extravagant and unforgettable new ways.

The title story, "Fire."—written especially for this volume—is a harrowing postapocalyptic adventure in a world threatened by global conflagration. Based on Hand's real-life experience as a participant in a governmental climate change think tank, it follows a ragtag cadre of scientists and artists racing to save both civilization and themselves from fast-moving global fires.

"The Woman Men Didn't See" is an expansion of Hand's acclaimed critical assessment of author Alice Sheldon, who wrote award-winning SF as "James Tiptree, Jr." in order to conceal identity from both the SF community and her CIA overlords. Another nonfiction piece, "Beyond Belief," recounts her difficult passage from alienated teen to serious artist.

Also included are "Kronia," a poignant time-travel romance, and "The Saffron Gatherers," two of Hand's favorite and less familiar stories. Plus: a bibliography and our candid and illuminating Outspoken Interview with one of today's most inventive authors.

Totalitopia

John Crowley
$14.00
ISBN: 978-1-62963-392-3
5x7.5 • 128 pages

John Crowley's all-new essay "Totalitopia" is a wry how-to guide for building utopias out of the leftovers of modern science fiction. "This Is Our Town," written especially for this volume, is a warm, witty, and wonderfully moving story about angels, cousins, and natural disasters based on a parochial school third-grade reader. One of Crowley's hard-to-find masterpieces, "Gone" is a Kafkaesque science fiction adventure about an alien invasion that includes door-to-door leafleting and yard work. Perhaps the most entertaining of Crowley's "Easy Chair" columns in *Harper's*, "Everything That Rises" explores the fractal interface between Russian spiritualism and quantum singularities—with a nod to both Columbus and Flannery O'Connor. "And Go Like This" creeps in from Datlow's Year's Best, the Wild Turkey of horror anthologies.

Plus: There's a bibliography, an author bio, and of course our Outspoken Interview, the usual cage fight between candor and common sense.

"Like a magus, John Crowley shares his secrets generously, allowing us to believe that his book is revealing the true and glorious nature of the world, and the reader's own place within it."
—Village Voice

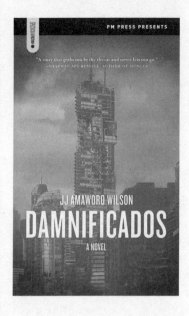

Damnificados

JJ Amaworo Wilson
$15.95
ISBN: 978-1-62963-117-2
5 by 8 • 288 pages

Damnificados is loosely based on the real-life occupation of a half-completed skyscraper in Caracas, Venezuela, the Tower of David. In this fictional version, six hundred "damnificados"—vagabonds and misfits—take over an abandoned urban tower and set up a community complete with schools, stores, beauty salons, bakeries, and a ragtag defensive militia. Their always heroic (and often hilarious) struggle for survival and dignity pits them against corrupt police, the brutal military, and the tyrannical "owners."

Taking place in an unnamed country at an unspecified time, the novel has elements of magical realism: avenging wolves, biblical floods, massacres involving multilingual ghosts, arrow showers falling to the tune of Beethoven's Ninth, and a trash truck acting as a Trojan horse. The ghosts and miracles woven into the narrative are part of a richly imagined world in which the laws of nature are constantly stretched and the past is always present.

> "Should be read by every politician and rich bastard and
> then force-fed to them—literally, page by page."
> —*Jimmy Santiago Baca, author of* A Place to Stand

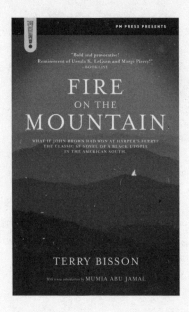

Fire on the Mountain

**Terry Bisson with an Introduction
by Mumia Abu-Jamal**
$15.95
ISBN: 978-1-60486-087-0
5 by 8 • 208 pages

It's 1959 in socialist Virginia. The Deep
South is an independent Black nation
called Nova Africa. The second Mars
expedition is about to touch down on
the red planet. And a pregnant scientist
is climbing the Blue Ridge in search of
her great-great grandfather, a teenage
slave who fought with John Brown
and Harriet Tubman's guerrilla army.

Long unavailable in the U.S., published in France as *Nova Africa*, *Fire on the
Mountain* is the story of what might have happened if John Brown's raid on
Harper's Ferry had succeeded—and the Civil War had been started not by
the slave owners but the abolitionists.

> *"History revisioned, turned inside out ... Bisson's
> wild and wonderful imagination has taken some
> strange turns to arrive at such a destination."*
> —Madison Smartt Bell, Anisfield-Wolf Award
> winner and author of Devil's Dream